This was her wedding.

The man beside her—he was practically a stranger—was going to be her husband. She told herself everything was all right. She told herself she was doing the right thing. She told herself she was doing the *best* thing.

When the time came to say her wedding vows, she said them from her heart. "I, Gina, take thee, Clay…"

Then Clay gazed into her eyes, and she wasn't so sure what she saw in his. The desire had vanished. His expression was somber, his voice deep, as he made his promise. "I, Clay, take thee, Gina…"

She'd said her vows, he'd said his. She had just promised to love Clay forever.

Was this a forever-promise for Clay, too, or was he simply promising to stay married to her for a year?

Dear Reader,

With summer nearly here, it's time to stock up on essentials such as sunblock, sandles and plenty of Silhouette Romance novels! Here's our checklist of page-turners to keep your days sizzling!

❏ *A Princess in Waiting* by Carol Grace (SR #1588)—In this ROYALLY WED: THE MISSING HEIR title, dashing Charles Rodin saves the day by marrying his brother's pregnant ex-wife!

❏ *Because of the Ring* by Stella Bagwell (SR #1589)—With this magical SOULMATES title, her grandmother's ring leads Claudia Westfield to the man of her dreams....

❏ *A Date with a Billionaire* by Julianna Morris (SR #1590)— Bethany Cox refused her prize—a date with the charitable Kane O'Rourke—but how can she get a gorgeous billionaire to take no for an answer? And does she really want to...?

❏ *The Marriage Clause* by Karen Rose Smith (SR #1591)— In this VIRGIN BRIDES installment, innocent Gina Foster agrees to a marriage of convenience with the wickedly handsome Clay McCormick, only to be swept into a world of passion.

❏ *The Man with the Money* by Arlene James (SR #1592)— A millionaire playboy in disguise romances a lovely foster mom. But will the truth destroy his chance at true love?

❏ *The 15 lb. Matchmaker* by Jill Limber (SR #1593)— Griff Price is the ultimate lone cowboy—until he's saddled with a baby and a jilted-bride-turned-nanny.

Be sure to come back next month for our list of great summer stories.

Happy reading!

Mary-Theresa Hussey
Senior Editor

Please address questions and book requests to:
Silhouette Reader Service
U.S.: 3010 Walden Ave., P.O. Box 1325, Buffalo, NY 14269
Canadian: P.O. Box 609, Fort Erie, Ont. L2A 5X3

The Marriage Clause

KAREN ROSE SMITH

SILHOUETTE *Romance*®

Published by Silhouette Books

America's Publisher of Contemporary Romance

To my aunt Rose Marie who lived the Alaskan life. With deepest appreciation to my indispensable Alaskan contacts—Sue Zawadzki and Wendy Ferguson. Thanks also to Wendy's husband, Doug, and Paul Arcuri, pilots and adventurers. Thank you all.

 SILHOUETTE BOOKS

ISBN 0-373-19591-5

THE MARRIAGE CLAUSE

Visit Silhouette at www.eHarlequin.com

Printed in U.S.A.

Books by Karen Rose Smith

Silhouette Romance

*Adam's Vow #1075
*Always Daddy #1102
*Shane's Bride #1128
†Cowboy at the Wedding #1171
†Most Eligible Dad #1174
†A Groom and a Promise #1181
The Dad Who Saved
   Christmas #1267
‡Wealth, Power and a
   Proper Wife #1320
‡ Love, Honor and a
   Pregnant Bride #1326
‡Promises, Pumpkins and
   Prince Charming #1332

The Night Before Baby #1348
‡Wishes, Waltzes and a Storybook
   Wedding #1407
Just the Man She Needed #1434
Just the Husband She Chose #1455
Her Honor-Bound Lawman #1480
Be My Bride? #1492
Tall, Dark & True #1506
Her Tycoon Boss #1523
Doctor in Demand #1536
A Husband in Her Eyes #1577
The Marriage Clause #1591

Silhouette Special Edition

Abigail and Mistletoe #930
The Sheriff's Proposal #1074
His Little Girl's Laughter #1426

Silhouette Books

The Fortunes of Texas
Marry in Haste...

*Darling Daddies
†The Best Men
‡ Do You Take This Stranger?

Previously published under the pseudonym Kari Sutherland

Silhouette Romance

Heartfire, Homefire #973

Silhouette Special Edition

Wish on the Moon #741

KAREN ROSE SMITH

is a former teacher and home decorator. Now spinning stories and creating characters keeps her busy. But she also loves listening to music, shopping and sharing with friends, as well as spending time with her son and her husband. Married for thirty years, she and her husband have always called Pennsylvania home. Karen Rose likes to hear from readers. Visit her Web site at www.karenrosesmith.com.

VIRGIN BRIDES

Celebrate the joys of first love

Dear Reader,

My husband and I celebrated our thirtieth wedding anniversary this year. Although many years have passed, I still remember our wedding day as vividly as if it were yesterday. I was filled with the same spine-tingling excitement, hopes, dreams and nervousness as my heroine. I remember my mother's hug as we stood in the vestibule of the church, my father's solemnity as he walked me down the aisle, my sense of belonging when I reached my husband-to-be at the altar.

When a woman marries the man she loves, her future stretches before her like a wonderful magic carpet. She has to take the ascents and dips in stride, at times hold on tight to her husband and the carpet, close her eyes and depend on faith to truly enjoy the journey. I've felt the tummy-tumbling hills and valleys, held on for dear life, and sometimes blindly let my heart lead. I can't imagine a more fulfilling thirty years.

I still believe in the power of love, and I want to thank my readers for believing in it with me.

All my best,

Karen Rose Smith

Chapter One

Why had his father done this to him?

Clay McCormick parked his SUV at the side entrance to the lodge and slammed the driver's door, knowing his anger wouldn't solve anything...knowing it wouldn't change the terms of his father's will. Leaves from alder, aspen and birch covered the ground while a few strays hung on to the branches. There had been a few heavy frosts and only light snow so far. October in Alaska could bring either a leisurely or an abrupt entry into the long winter. Clay loved the winters as much as he loved the rest of the year in Alaska. He'd been forced to leave as a boy, but he'd returned as a teenager and had no desire to set foot Outside again.

The frosty breeze ruffled his shaggy brown hair as he looked up at the three-story lodge he and his father had made a success. They'd been partners in a flying service first. Then as his dad had neared sixty, they'd invested in this lodge. John McCormick had run it like the business expert he was, while Clay had devoted most of his time to the flying service.

Now he could lose everything.

Unless he married.

Marriage. He'd sworn he'd never make those promises again. He'd vowed that just like his father, it was better to spend life alone, flying the skies over the last primitive territory of the United States, than to again put his heart into a woman's hands.

His father had needed a woman with a pioneer spirit, but the long cold winters and loneliness had led his mother to drink and then to leave. The only problem was—she'd dragged Clay with her. He'd resented being taken from his father and a place he loved. Unfortunately, he hadn't learned from his father's mistake and his own marriage had lasted less than a year for the same reasons.

So, damn it all! Why had John McCormick made marriage a condition for Clay to claim his inheritance? Since his divorce, he hadn't dated much. He'd been too bitter for that. There'd been one woman who'd sparked his interest, but she hadn't been free.

The heavy wooden door on the side entrance to the lodge creaked as he pushed it open and stepped inside. The first floor consisted of the dining room, a large sitting room and a main office. That's where he headed now, past the wide stairway that led to the second and third floors. Suddenly he heard a sweet, lilting voice float down from the second floor.

"Just ring the main office if you need anything, Mr. Habersham. Dinner is at six. I'll see you then."

Before Clay could take another step, Gina Foster descended the stairs with a grace and energy that always made him want to stop and watch her. His dad had hired her to manage the lodge. Clay hadn't approved of his father's choice, and it had nothing to do with his blood racing faster and his body going on alert every time he looked into Gina's wide blue eyes or saw her black curls bob around her heart-shaped face. It had to do with her inexperience and her youth and a quality about her he hadn't seen much in women these days—innocence. For all those reasons, he'd stayed away from her. Yet he had to admit, she'd done a damn fine job of running the lodge.

She reached the landing and only lighted there a moment before she descended the rest of the steps and asked him, "What's wrong? Didn't your meeting with your father's attorney go well?"

He'd always considered himself quite good at hiding his emotions. That she could read him now told him exactly how disturbed he was about what he'd learned in the lawyer's office. "You won't believe what Dad put in his will."

At five-five, Gina had to look up a good seven inches to meet his eyes. There was a shy quality about her voice as she asked softly, "Your father's will was different than you expected?"

The gentleness in her voice, the cornflower-blue of the corduroy dress that fell softly over her breasts, defining her very small waist and falling almost to the calves of her beautifully curved legs, distracted him for a moment. But only for a moment.

Anger overrode the grief that had been with him whether he was awake or sleeping over the past two weeks since his dad had died. "I never expected terms like these. If I didn't know better, I'd say he was out of his mind when he made this will."

She came a few steps closer. "Your father was clearheaded to the very last."

"I know. That's what makes this so crazy. C'mon. Let's go into the office. I'd better fill you in because this is going to affect you, too."

She looked surprised at that, as if she didn't see how that was possible.

After they stepped into the pine-paneled office, Clay unzipped his leather jacket and waved to the lodgepole-pine settee with its brown plaid cushions. They sat side by side, arms almost brushing. Desire stirred inside of him as the scent of Gina's shampoo or perfume or something delicate and sweet made it impossible for him to think. Shifting a couple of inches away from her, he cleared his throat and told himself—as he had for months—that her hair couldn't possibly be as soft as it looked.

Then he recalled again everything his lawyer had told him. "This is the bottom line," he said gruffly. "I have to marry within three months and stay married—defined as under the same roof—for a year in order to keep the lodge and the flying service. If I don't meet the terms of the will, all of it will be sold and the money will be donated to a wildlife preservation fund."

"Oh, Clay!" She looked as horrified as he felt.

He'd been fighting his attraction to Gina ever since they'd hired her. That, as well as the turmoil of the whole preposterous concept, pushed him to his feet. The sound of his boots on the plank flooring as he strode to the window echoed in the silence. He looked out over land and spruce and fence line that soon would be snow-covered. The lodge was located a half hour out of Fairbanks on fifteen acres of the most beautiful property on this earth. The house he'd built last year nestled into the firs, not far away. It was a log home, built with permanence in mind. Now he might lose that, too.

No way in hell.

"Clay, you're sure there isn't some mistake?" Gina asked, obvious concern in her voice. "Mr. Mc-Cormick couldn't have done that to you. He wasn't that kind of man. He loved you."

Clay was as sure that his father had loved him as he was that Gina had been raised to respect her elders. His father had wanted her to call him John, but she never could bring herself to do it. He'd been Mr. Mc-Cormick until she'd held his hand and said her last goodbye. Clay's gaze had met hers the moment after that and he'd felt so much, including a bond with her that had gone way beyond an employer-employee relationship. He'd attributed it to everything he was feeling about the loss of his father.

Turning away from the window, he met her beautiful blue eyes. "Dad meant it, Gina. That's what I can't understand. The will is clear and uncontestable, according to his lawyer."

The phone rang shrilly then, interrupting a discussion that was only beginning.

Clay went to the desk and snatched up the receiver, hoping beyond hope that it was the attorney saying there had been some mistake.

"Clay, it's Greg. Thank goodness I found you. I got voice-mail on your cell. Then I called the hangar—"

Greg Savard had been a friend of Clay's since they were teenagers. While Clay had taken courses in business management, gotten his pilot's license, instrument rating and then commercial certification, Greg had attended med school. He'd gone Outside to Washington State for his training, but he'd come back and opened his practice in Fairbanks. He'd found Mary Lou when she'd applied for a job as a receptionist in his office and now he had three kids. He was a lucky man.

Normally even-tempered, Clay heard a note in his friend's voice now that was unusual. "What's up?" he asked.

"It's Tanner. He got into a fight at school, and Mary Lou grounded him until I got home. He must have snuck out of the house. None of his friends have seen him and I found his footprints leading into the woods." Greg's voice broke. "I've been searching with neighbors for an hour, and we can't find him—"

Tanner was nine years old, Greg's firstborn. Clay had never heard the kind of terrified panic in his friend's voice that he heard now, and he knew what Greg wanted him to do. Yet spotting a child from the air wouldn't be easy. Still, if luck was with him... "I'll call Dave and tell him to fire up the Seneca. We'll be in the air as fast as I can manage it. Call me on the cell if you hear anything until I get going."

"Thanks, Clay."

"We'll find him." As Clay settled the receiver on the desk, he prayed his words of assurance would come true.

"That was Dr. Savard?" Gina asked. She'd met Greg when he'd come to the lodge several times to check on Clay's dad.

"Tanner got mad and took off. He's only nine and Greg and Mary Lou are panicked."

"Is there anything I can do?"

For a few valuable seconds, Clay studied her. "Mary Lou doesn't have any family here. With Greg's parents gone now... Would you be willing to handle her phone and organize what's going on at the house? You're good at that."

Gina blinked in surprise at the compliment. "Everything here is under control. With the season slowing down, we only have three guests for dinner. Joanie can act as hostess as well as waitress. I'm sure she won't mind."

"Okay. You tell her what's up. I'll bring the car around to the front so you can hop in when you're ready. There's no time to spare."

As Gina nodded and left the room, her black curls bobbed over her dress collar and the sway of her hips made Clay's gut clench.

The pretty lodge manager was twenty-three years old and had lived in San Francisco until she'd come to Alaska. As Clay had told his father when he'd hired her, she'd never last. She'd come to Alaska on a whim...for an adventure. That kind of woman left when the nights grew twenty hours long and the temperature dropped to forty below.

Yet every time Clay came in contact with her, his desire for her became a little more intense.

His jaw clenched when he thought again about his father's will. Then he went to get his SUV.

Less than a foot from Clay in his SUV, Gina could feel the tension in him and his eagerness to be up in his plane, searching for his friend's son. She'd learned a great deal about Clay McCormick in the past six months. Not because of the amount of time she'd spent with him. She hadn't spent much time with him at all. Yet difficult circumstances brought out both the best and worst in everyone. Even in her twenty-three years she'd learned that.

After John McCormick had hired her, she'd felt Clay's protective consideration for his father. Clay had explained about his dad's declining health and told her he was counting on her to take the burden of lodge management from his father. He'd asked her point-blank if she was experienced enough to do that. Right then and there she'd learned Clay McCormick was honest and direct. At the time, she hadn't known if she'd been experienced enough. Because of *her* father, she didn't know very much about life. Still, she'd told Clay she'd try her best and that had seemed to satisfy him.

Over the next few months she'd watched Clay tend to his father as he'd gone through chemotherapy and radiation. She'd heard the arguments when Clay tried to convince his dad to go to Seattle for an experimental treatment. John McCormick had told his son he wasn't leaving Fairbanks. He'd take the time he had left and do the most he could with it. That day she'd seen the resignation in Clay and felt his frustration. He was a pilot who wanted to control his world and his destiny. Losing his father hadn't been part of that. Yet he'd accepted his dad's wishes, hired a day nurse toward the end, and sat through the night shifts himself. There was no doubt that Clay faced life's challenges head-on.

She didn't. She'd run away from San Francisco, and her father, and a wedding she didn't want because it was the only way she could see to escape. Clay would never respect her if he knew about all that. He'd think she was a coward.

Was she still?

She didn't know. What she did know was that she was mightily attracted to this man sitting beside her... but he was way out of her reach.

"Are you sure your friends won't think I'm intruding?" she asked now.

"Having second thoughts about helping out?"

"No, but I'm sure the little boy's mother is distraught—"

"Mary Lou might be distraught, but she's a strong woman. I called her and asked her if she could use your help. She's grateful because she's dealing with two search parties. If nothing else, you can give her a hand keeping hot coffee going. I don't have time to do more than drop you at the door. Are you okay with that?"

He glanced at her with a look that said he expected her to live up to this challenge just as she'd lived up to the challenge of running the lodge. She always felt shy with Clay, and she knew that made him look at her as if she was even younger and more inexperienced than she was.

"I'll be fine. Did you say your friends had two other children?"

"Yes. Noelle's almost three and Bobby's five."

"I can always keep *them* occupied."

This time, Clay's brown gaze was curious as it fell on her. "You like kids?"

"When I was at boarding school, I volunteered on weekends in the pediatrics ward. I'm really good with puppets," she said with a reassuring smile.

The lines around Clay's eyes seemed to relax just for a few moments as he almost smiled back. "I'll keep that in mind. When the long nights set in, maybe you can keep us both entertained.''

She'd read about the long Alaskan nights, the sub-zero winter cold. It would be different than anything she'd ever experienced. Yet wasn't that why she'd answered John McCormick's ad? Wasn't that why she'd left a pampered life and overprotective father as well as a man who wanted to marry her for his own gain? Coming to Alaska had been her way of finding independence and who she really was.

When Clay pulled up in front of Mary Lou and Greg's ranch-style house, Gina unbuckled her seat belt.

Before she could open her door, Clay reached out and clasped her arm. ''Thanks for helping.''

She knew it was impossible, but it was as though she could feel the heat of his hand through her rose-colored down parka. As she gazed into his dark brown eyes, she wondered if her dreams of kissing Clay McCormick could be anything close to the reality.

Then she remembered that he'd been married and divorced. He was eleven years older than she was. What did she have to offer him?

''No thanks necessary,'' she murmured, opened the door, and hopped out before she did or said something foolish.

When Mary Lou Savard opened her front door, Clay drove off.

Gina gazed into the face of a woman around the same age as Clay. Her cheeks were tear-streaked, and Gina could only begin to understand how this mother felt. ''I'm Gina Foster. I'm here to help any way I can.''

* * *

Clay's right-hand man at the hangar had the Piper Seneca II ready for takeoff. Clay owned two twin-engine planes, the Seneca and a Cessna Skymaster. Paul Simmons, a pilot he'd hired when he'd taken over running the air service, usually flew the Cessna. His maintenance chief, Dave Wagner, took care of the planes and the hangar. He was Clay's all-around man-Friday and would ride with Clay, searching for Tanner as well as watching the sky for other aircraft and electrical lines. Since spotting the boy from the air would be difficult, two pairs of eyes were definitely better than one.

After a quick run-through to make sure Dave had covered all the bases, they were in the plane, on the runway, then soaring up into Clay's idea of perfection. There was nothing that compared with flying, absolutely nothing at all. Not even sex.

Gina Foster's face popped up in front of his eyes, and he tried to blank it out. He didn't need that distraction while he was searching for Tanner.

Veering toward the woods behind Greg's house, he spoke into his headset to Dave. "Tanner's wearing a red-and-blue jacket with a red ski cap."

"Got it," the russet-haired maintenance man said with a thumbs-up sign.

With the hum of the plane's engines around him, Clay took three wide passes over the area, scanning the landscape for a little boy who was already rebelling against authority.

Although he focused on flying and finding Tanner, Clay could still hear his father's lawyer's voice ringing in his ears above the sound of the engines. *You must marry within three months and stay legitimately married a full year in order to receive your inheritance. Otherwise, you will lose everything.*

With Greg's call, Clay had tried to put the meeting with the attorney into the back of his head. But it wouldn't stay there. Again Gina's face became clear in his mind's eye and he realized a crazy idea had nudged into his thoughts—*Consider marrying Gina.*

His heart pounded, and he told himself not to be ridiculous. She was eleven years younger than he was. She'd never even been through an Alaskan winter! The fog in San Francisco was a far cry from the fierce wind, blizzards and never-ending nights.

So who else can you ask? A voice inside his head persisted.

There wasn't anyone else. He hadn't dated much since his divorce. He'd been most interested in a sexy pilot he'd met in Juneau. But he'd discovered even though she was separated, she'd still been entangled with her husband.

Damn it, Dad. Why did you do this to me?

Before he even considered waiting for an answer, he thought he caught a glimpse of red and blue against a patch of snow near the base of a foothill. He quickly circled the area once more and saw the flash of red and blue again, pointing it out to Dave. With a great sigh of relief, he realized they'd found Tanner.

Picking up the radio, he called in the information to the search parties. Then he kept an eye on the boy, intending to keep track of him until the searchers found him.

When Clay returned to Greg and Mary Lou's house, no one heard his knock, but Clay could hear the chatter inside. He opened the door and found the living room full of people, probably the neighbors who'd been looking for Tanner. Greg was passing out mugs of hot coffee while Mary Lou sat on the sofa, Tanner beside her in the crook of her arm wrapped in a blanket, sipping from a mug. To his surprise, Clay saw Gina on the sofa, too. She was holding Noelle, helping her drink from a child-sized cup. Bobby was nestled in on her other side, holding a book he obviously wanted her to read. Apparently she *did* like children, and they liked her.

As if some sixth sense told her he'd entered the room, she looked up and saw him. Her shy smile wrapped around Clay's heart, and he felt his body stirring with a primitive response that had become bothersome whenever he was around her. Now he wondered about that response. He wondered about an idea that seemed totally insane.

Mary Lou spotted Clay, hopped up from the sofa, and ran toward him giving him a huge hug. "We can never repay you for what you did," she said, her eyes filling with tears.

"Anyone with a plane could have done what I did."

She shook her head. "You're a wonderful friend, Clay. Gina has been such a help, too. She's so good with the kids. While I kept in touch with the search parties and made coffee and sandwiches, she kept Noelle and Bobby busy. They could see how worried I was, and she helped keep everything on an even keel."

Greg came over to him then and pounded him on the back. "I always knew having a friend who flies his own plane would come in handy sometime."

"So that's why we stayed friends all these years," Clay jibed.

"Must be," Greg answered, his voice husky.

They never talked about what their friendship meant. Words weren't necessary. Now words would only stir up emotion they were both trying to keep in check.

Motioning to the table laden with sandwiches and a bag of chips and drinks, Mary Lou suggested, "Come have something to eat."

Too much was weighing on his shoulders for him to make casual conversation. "Gina and I really should be getting back. I have to make some calls, and she'll want to make sure the guests at the lodge are settled in for the night."

Mary Lou nodded, understanding. Going over to the sofa, she held her hands out to her daughter and lifted Noelle from Gina's lap.

Clay crossed to Gina and asked, "Are you ready?"

When Bobby looked up at Gina, he wailed, "I wanted you to read me a story."

Gina ruffled the little boy's hair. "Maybe another time."

"Promise?" the five-year-old asked seriously.

Gina glanced up at Clay and then down at Bobby again. "I promise."

After Greg fetched Gina's parka, Clay took it from his friend and held it out for her. When she slipped her arm into it, she was very close to him. He was tempted to bend his head and let his chin feel the silk of her curls. As the thought passed through his mind, she looked up at him. He saw her lower lip tremble, but he couldn't be sure. Was she as aware of him as he was of her?

If this attraction was two-sided...

As they walked to the car, he reminded himself she would never stay in Alaska. Then he remembered the will stipulated a year. What if he made staying for that year worth her while? What if he offered her a sum of money too large for her to turn down? Neither of them would have to change their lives. They could easily live under one roof. His father had told him Gina was trying to build a nest egg to start her own business—a tea room. A lump sum of money could go a long way to doing that for her.

Once in the car, Gina said to Clay, "You did a wonderful thing for them today. I wish you could have been there to see Mary Lou take Tanner into her arms when the searchers brought him back. I don't think Greg knew whether he should throttle him or hug him to death."

"Tanner has a mind of his own. Just like his dad," Clay added with a grin. "Greg will have to get used to that. I'm sure he'll have a good talk with Tanner tonight about not running away when the going gets tough."

Gina went silent at that, and Clay glanced over at her. She looked sad and he wondered what that was all about. "It looked as if Bobby took a shine to you. He'll be disappointed if you don't read him a story."

"When I have some free time next week, I'll give Mary Lou a call. I have to keep my promise to him."

"Do you always keep your promises?"

"I try."

Gina's words kept Clay's mind occupied for the remainder of the drive. He didn't even realize they'd traveled the rest of the way in silence until he'd pulled up at the side entrance to the lodge.

He checked the clock on the dash. "There's something I'd like to discuss with you."

"I should check on the guests."

"The guests can wait. This is important, Gina. Let's go to the office."

She gazed at him steadily for a moment. "All right."

While he got out and went around to open her door, he thought about the terms of his father's will. He also thought about the years he'd put into building up the flying business and the lodge, his house on the property and his retirement account.

Gina was already out of the car and waiting for him on the path to the lodge. Snow began falling lightly as they walked the short distance. When Clay opened the door for Gina and let her precede him inside, she passed close by and he felt that stirring in his body again. He thought about his marriage and his divorce and how it had affected his life. As they walked down the hall, he knew he'd do just about anything to keep his life as he knew it—including a marriage of convenience for a year.

When they passed the sitting room, he heard male voices. He saw the glow of the fire in the hearth and realized one of the guests must have put match to tinder. The thought was fleeting as his mind settled on Gina and the question he was about to ask her.

She removed her parka, hanging it on the coatrack. Then she stood by the desk, waiting for him expectantly. He tossed his coat onto a spare wooden chair.

He wasn't sure where to begin, so he decided the best thing was just to begin. "I've been thinking about my father's will. I don't want to lose everything

I've spent the last fifteen years building. There's only one way to keep it all—I have to get married.''

She looked astonished and something else, too. But he couldn't read her well enough to know what emotion deepened the blue of her eyes.

"Who are you going to ask to marry you?" Her voice was soft and a bit tremulous.

He waited the span of a heartbeat, then answered, "You. Will you marry me, Gina?"

Chapter Two

Gina's heart pounded so hard she had to take a deep breath to calm herself. She must have heard Clay incorrectly. "You're asking *me* to marry you?"

His expression was as somber as she'd ever seen it. "Before you toss the idea out as totally ridiculous, listen to me. I have to marry within three months and stay married for a year. Finding a woman willing to do that isn't easy."

"So you're choosing me because it's an *easy* solution?" On one hand Clay was holding out to her something she'd thought she could never have. On the other…

"I'm handling this badly," he muttered. "This is the deal. I like you. I've been attracted to you since the first day I met you, and I think you feel the buzz between us, too. But I'm older and I haven't wanted to take advantage of you. I still don't. You're looking for your life. I've found mine. Still, I think I can offer you something that would make this worth your while. You told Dad you wanted to build up a nest egg to start your own business. A tea room, right?''

''Yes. A shop with gourmet coffees and teas, herbal products...with a tea room where I can have pastries for breakfast and high tea. It's a dream I've always had.''

''Think about making that dream come true. If you marry me and we stay married for a full year, I'll give you $50,000.''

She felt the color drain from her face. ''Where will you get that kind of money?'' she blurted out.

''Ever since I started working, I've made investments. Over the years it's turned into a tidy sum. If I meet the terms of the will and inherit the lodge and the flying service, that's all I'll need. Money doesn't mean that much to me. It's simply a necessity. What's important is holding on to this place and doing the work I love.''

After she thought about that, she considered everything he'd said. She could help him make his dreams come true.

What about her dreams?

Not just the tea room. Ever since she was a child, she'd read stories about princes who swept ordinary women off their feet and vowed undying love. The deal her father had arranged with Trent Jones, her lack of feelings for Trent, the absence of passion she believed had to be part of a marriage, had been the antithesis of her dream. That's why she'd run from it.

''Gina, I know this is coming way out of left field,'' Clay went on. ''But neither of us would have to change our lives that much. We'd be moving into my house. You'd still be working here, doing a job you seem to enjoy. You'd still receive your salary.''

He was being so very practical. Suddenly she knew she wanted so much more from Clay than practicality. She wanted two dreams instead of one. She realized now she had more than a crush on Clay McCormick. She'd been falling in love with him the whole time she'd been working at the lodge and hadn't even realized it.

Although they'd been standing only about two feet apart, now Clay came even closer. He looked down into her eyes as if he was trying to see everything inside her—who she was, who she might become, or if she could fit into his life.

Then slowly, he brought his large hand to her cheek and leisurely fingered a curl dangling by her ear. "So soft," he murmured.

She was mesmerized by the huskiness in his voice, the light of desire in his terrifically dark brown eyes. He said he'd been attracted to her since the first day he'd met her. She'd been attracted to him, too. More than attracted. Drawn. Excited whenever she was near him. His calloused hand on her cheek made every nerve ending inside of her tingle. She loved the feel of his fingers on her skin.

Her heart raced, her breath became quick and short, and when he bent his head and said in a low voice, "Let's experiment," she knew what swooning was all about. Yet she couldn't swoon because she wanted to remember and enjoy and revel in everything that was about to happen.

His mouth covered hers before she had time to think deeply about his words. For the past six months, she'd dreamt about kissing him. It had been an inexperienced girl's dream. Now she was a woman faced with reality. Clay was all man, all muscle and strength and sensual desire. When his lips covered hers with a mastery she expected but had never experienced, she knew she was way out of her depth. His mouth was firm and hot, demanding yet teasingly erotic.

The direct simplicity of the kiss didn't last long. His tongue slid along the seam of her lips. It took her a moment to realize he wanted her to open her mouth, to part her lips, to let him come in. She trembled at the thought of it and when she did it, his tongue quickened rivers of fire that heated her until she felt as if she'd go up in flames. Goodness sakes! Is this what kissing was all about? Trent had given her a good-night, end-of-evening, see-you-next-time kiss that hadn't excited her at all. He'd wanted her to open her mouth, too, and she had for a few seconds. It had been on their second date, and he'd laid his palm over her breast as if he'd had a right to do it. She'd ended that kiss and backed off, confused by everything she hadn't felt.

Now with Clay, she felt so much of everything— hot tingles, erotic thoughts, breathlessness, shaky knees that had her hanging on to his shoulders for dear life.

Then it was over. He was releasing her and lifting his head and staring down at her with an intensity that was almost as powerful as their kiss had been.

"That was a highly successful experiment," he concluded, his voice deep.

She knew she had to take her hands from his shoulders. They slipped to her sides when he put a good foot between them and suggested, "Think about everything I've said, Gina. Think about that kiss. Think about being married and what you could do with

$50,000. We'll discuss it tomorrow night over dinner. All right?''

Because she couldn't seem to find her voice, she simply nodded.

Before she had time to fill her lungs with a bolstering breath, he picked up his jacket and exited the office. She was left with her body thrumming from all the sensations his kiss had evoked. She was also confused about how her dreams could match up with reality.

After Gina had checked on dinner the following evening and the tables in the dining room, the mobile phone on her belt rang. She straightened a napkin on a table and answered, ''Hello. McCormick Lodge.''

''Gina?''

Clay's deep voice ran through her and she remembered their kiss last night. ''Hi, Clay.''

''I'm not going to get back for dinner tonight. I'm sorry. I had to fly around a front and arrived in Galena later than I expected. There are some clients here I need to see so I'll be staying overnight.''

''That's all right,'' she said, though it wasn't. They had their future to discuss. Maybe that wasn't so important to him anymore. Maybe he was already regretting his proposal. Maybe he realized exactly how inexperienced she was when he'd kissed her last night. After all, what did she have to offer him except signing her name on a marriage license?

''We'll talk when I get back tomorrow. This is something I couldn't help.''

''I understand.'' Part of her did. The other part of her wondered if he wasn't grateful they could postpone the discussion.

All evening Gina worried about it. To say she was insecure where men were concerned was an understatement. She'd attended an all-girls private academy in San Francisco until she was twelve. Then her father had sent her to boarding school—a fine boarding school with a wonderful reputation. It was as protective of its students as her father was of her. College hadn't been much different. Again at her father's urging, she'd kept her focus on her studies, a double major in French along with hotel and restaurant management. There hadn't been much time for a social life. Every semester she'd made the Dean's List to make her father proud.

Because Wesley Foster worked long hours and had tons of business commitments, she'd been raised by nannies after her mother died. Her goal in life had been to never cause her father any trouble and to appreciate any leftover moments he could give her. When she graduated from college and found a job at a bed and breakfast, her hours had been long. Although she'd intended to move out of her childhood home eventually, she'd stayed so she could see her dad as much as possible.

Then Trent Jones had asked her out and after they'd dated a few times, he was talking about a summer wedding. Her father had heartily approved and actually began wedding preparations, renting a ballroom in a hotel. It was then she'd realized she had no say in her life. She'd had a talk with her dad about not loving Trent, but he hadn't paid any attention to her. She wondered if he ever really had. It was like talking to a brick wall, and Trent wasn't much better. Finally she'd realized why.

This past March she'd overheard her father and

Trent talking. Trent wanted a written document from her father assuring his promotion and signing bonus as soon as he married her. Her father had agreed. In the hall to the parlor, she'd been mortified. Did her father think she couldn't find her own husband? Did Trent have any feelings at all for her? Or was she simply a stepping stone? At that moment, she'd decided to put both men out of her life, to find her own future and carve her own course. Somehow she'd gotten through her date with Trent that night.

The next day she'd gone over want ads in major newspapers, needing to get as far away from San Francisco as she could. That's when she'd seen John McCormick's ad, that's when she'd headed into the unknown with only her savings from working the past two years. She'd left her father a note saying she'd be fine and he shouldn't worry. After she'd gotten the job in Fairbanks, she'd sent him a letter via a guest, who'd mailed it from Seattle. She hadn't trusted him with her location until summer. Immediately he'd flown to Fairbanks to meet her, intent on taking her home. He hadn't even wanted to see the lodge. For the first time in her life, she'd stood up to him. She'd told him she was staying and there was nothing he could say or do to change her mind. That day she'd finally felt like an adult.

He still called her every few weeks, still tried to convince her to come back to San Francisco. She was determined to stay. She was determined to choose her own future.

Now she had to decide whether or not she wanted her future to include a marriage to Clay McCormick.

It was after six when Clay returned the following day. Gina wasn't in the dining room where she usually circulated while their guests dined. Joanie, a middle-aged brunette who'd been a waitress at the lodge since it had opened, told him, "She's cooking tonight. I'll let *her* tell you why."

When Clay entered the kitchen, it smelled richly of beef and he immediately saw Gina, the chef's apron tied double around her waist as she dished vegetables onto the platters.

"Where's Richard?"

"He quit. Two weeks early. He found a position as a sous-chef in one of the best restaurants in Fairbanks. He said he couldn't turn it down. They needed him to start immediately or they'd find somebody else."

"So he just left us in the lurch?"

"Not exactly. I agreed to let him go. I can cook, Clay. Besides management courses, I had cooking classes. We only have the three guests, and they'll be leaving at the end of the week. There are no bookings for next week, so it seemed reasonable to let Richard go."

Bustling in just then, Joanie picked up the round tray with the three platters and hurried back out. Clay liked the attractive waitress who was dating his mechanic. She was discreet.

Clay noticed the peach pastry sitting on the counter. "You made that?"

"Sure did. Thank goodness for canned goods. What I wouldn't give for a real fruit pie."

There were conveniences Alaskans just didn't have because of the cost of having products flown in. Fresh fruit this time of year was one of them. Gina's comment made him wonder what other conveniences and advantages she missed.

That brought him to the discussion they had to have. "Do you want to join me for a late dinner?"

She avoided his gaze and opened one of the cutlery drawers. "I don't know if I'll have time. I spent most of the afternoon in the kitchen. After I serve the guests, I have to clean up and then make sure they don't need anything else tonight."

Clay felt more was going on here than busyness. Gina was avoiding her meeting with him. He was too proud to push it. He certainly wasn't going to beg her to marry him. If it wasn't in the cards, he'd come up with another solution. Yet recalling the feel of Gina's hair in his fingers, her inexperienced kiss that had fired his blood, he was in more turmoil about the whole thing than he wanted to admit.

"I'll be upstairs in my father's office if you want to talk later. If you don't have time, we'll do it tomorrow." Then he left the kitchen and headed for the stairs and his father's apartment on the third floor.

The third floor of the lodge contained four small suites. Each had a bedroom, a sitting room and a bath. Two of them they rented out. Clay had lived in one until he'd built his house, and his father had lived in the other. When they'd hired Gina, she'd taken Clay's old suite.

The sitting room of John McCormick's suite was more office than lounging area. A small TV and recliner, bookshelves and a massive desk took up most of the room. Clay hadn't been through his father's possessions yet and didn't know if he'd ever be ready to do it. Soon he did have to sort through all the pertinent business information and tax records. Still, as he entered his father's quarters, this was the one place where he could really feel his father's presence. Clay crossed the room and sank down into his dad's aged red-leather chair. It creaked as it always did.

Scanning the photographs on one wall, Clay focused on one of him and his dad standing in front of the Seneca. His high school graduation picture hung next to an enlarged photo of the view from Glacier Bay, as well as an aerial view of Fairbanks and another of the lodge on the first day they opened for business.

Clay leaned back in the chair and stared at the photo of his father. "Why'd you do it, Dad?" he asked again. "Why did you write such a will?"

This time he almost expected an answer.

Of course, there still wasn't one. He might never have the answer. Opening the desk drawer, he pulled out several folders and laid them on the desk.

He wasn't sure how long he'd been going through papers when there was a soft rap at the door. He looked up and saw Gina. When she gave him a tentative smile, he wanted to kiss her all over again.

"Do you still want to talk?" she asked.

Standing, he crossed to the sofa and motioned to it. She came in and sat beside him…a good six inches away.

She said, "I have a question."

Looking into her blue eyes, he thought he'd never seen a color so clearly beautiful. "Go ahead."

"What would you expect from a marriage?" Her cheeks reddened.

"Does this mean you're considering my proposal seriously?"

She evaded him. "I need to know the...conditions first."

"A marriage of convenience should have advantages, don't you think? The will stipulates we have to live under the same roof. It's a possibility we could just be housemates."

He paused, studying her face, trying to gauge her thoughts. Deciding it was easier to read her reactions than her thoughts, he brought his hand up to her lips and rubbed his thumb along the bottom one. She trembled.

"Then again," he went on, continuing his train of thought, "I want you, Gina." He rubbed his finger across her lower lip again. "Do you want me?"

"Can't...can't you tell?" she asked in almost a whisper.

"I need you to say it. I need to know we're clear on what's happening between us. I won't coerce you into anything you don't want. But if we marry, I want you in my bed."

He saw the flutter of her pulse at her throat, the quickening of her breath, the rise and fall of her breasts. "I want you, Clay, but it's not that... simple."

"Why not?"

"What if we have children? What if it doesn't work out? Even if we're careful, there's always the chance that birth control might fail."

Still too clearly, Clay could remember being torn away from his father...torn away from Alaska. If he had a child, he would want him or her to inherit not only the lodge but a sense of history, appreciation for this land and then the courage to deal with it. "My parents divorced when I was nine because my mother hated it here. She took me to Illinois with her where her family was. *I* hated that. I never wanted to leave my father and live Outside. If by some accident you and I did have children and you decide to leave Alaska, you have to agree to give me custody. I won't give up my son or daughter the way my father did.''

Her wide blue eyes searched his face. ''That's a serious stipulation.''

''I know it is. But it's one I have to make.''

''You're making my decision more difficult.''

Clay ran his hand through his hair. ''Alaska's in my blood and in a way, it's my life. The McCormicks have lived here for four generations. My father might have been able to prolong his life if he'd gone to Seattle for treatment, but he wouldn't leave here and wanted to die here. I feel the same way. It's impossible to explain if you don't know Alaska. If we marry, maybe I can teach you all about it.''

He found himself wanting to do that, hoping that Gina could put down roots here with him. Didn't he know better? Hadn't Elizabeth proven to him that women with a pioneer spirit were few and far between?

''I know you want an answer,'' Gina finally said. ''Now that I know all the terms, I have to think about this a bit more. Can you give me time?''

If Gina didn't accept his proposal, he had to figure out what he'd do next. ''I can give you a week.''

When she nodded solemnly and answered, ''A week it is,'' he felt her sincerity. There were no games with her, no practiced flirting. Her innocence was seductive. He was close enough to her to tip her chin up and kiss her. Instead, he decided he didn't want to use the chemistry bubbling between them to convince her. This marriage had to be based on practicality and reason.

He leaned away from her. "Will you need help with breakfast since Richard's gone?"

She blinked as if not expecting the sudden change of subject, as if she'd been expecting his kiss. He almost smiled. Better if they both wanted it and waited for it.

"I...guess so. Richard was adept at having three things going at once. It would be nice having someone keep an eye on the bacon while I cook the eggs."

"All right. I'll meet you in the kitchen around six-thirty."

He realized he wanted to spend time around her. He wanted to see if she was as sweet as she seemed. They both needed to go into this with their eyes open.

A few moments after Gina left his dad's office, he heard the door to her suite close. Instead of returning to the papers on his father's desk, Clay went over to the bookshelf and found himself studying the titles. Many were books about the history of Alaska. One well-used leather bound volume caught his eye, and he pulled it from the shelf. When he opened it, he realized it was a diary. On the dotted line on the front page in strong well-formed letters, he read, *Alfred McCormick.*

Flipping through the pages, Clay found it was a journal of his grandfather's life. The first date was February 17, 1928. The entry read:

> I met the woman of my dreams this evening—
> Cora Johnson. Though she doesn't know it yet,
> I'm going to marry her. She told me life is a
> great adventure and she's ready to start on it.

She's traveled all the way from Pennsylvania to teach school in Fairbanks. Now all I have to do is court her and persuade her I can support her with my trapping and trading.

Though Clay was tempted to read on, he closed the journal and decided to take it back to the house with him. He had to look over his schedule for the next few days and check preliminary weather reports. The journal and the reports would be a good distraction to keep him from thinking about Gina's answer to his proposal.

When Clay met Gina in the kitchen the following morning, there was a definite tension between them. They might have a future together, or they might not. Basically, they were strangers, thinking about taking the next steps in life's journey together. He told himself he could ignore the chemistry between them but as his gaze met Gina's, it was as tangible as the propane flames beneath the bacon he was frying.

As she scrambled the eggs, he tried to make conversation to learn more about her. "I know you're from San Francisco. Did you always live there?"

Scrambling took on new meaning as Gina whipped the eggs into a frenzy. "Yes, all my life."

"Then your relatives are there."

Her whisk slowed a bit. "I don't have many relatives. My mother died when I was seven." Wistfully she added, "I can barely remember her now. Mostly I remember photographs I've seen of her."

"I'm sorry," Clay said simply, meaning it. After a few moments of silence, he asked, "Your dad still lives in San Francisco?"

"Oh, yes."

Something in Gina's tone made Clay look at her more closely. "You and your dad don't get along?"

She hesitated a few moments, then finally admitted, "We get along just fine as long as I do exactly what he says. I did that for twenty-three years until I took the job up here."

Before Clay could question Gina further about her father, the kitchen door swung open and one of the guests came in. He was the youngest of the three men staying at the lodge—around Gina's age, Clay supposed. He was good-looking in a GQ kind of way. He had business in Fairbanks and had chosen to stay at the lodge rather than in town.

Tim Bennett nodded at Clay, but his smile was for Gina. "I didn't know if I'd see you again this morning. I'll be out all day and won't be back until this evening. I wanted to tell you how much I enjoyed dinner last night. I knew you had to take over as chef. Joanie told me. The meal was terrific."

Gina looked surprised at the compliment. "Thank you, Tim. I enjoyed making it. What are you doing today?"

"I'm setting up computers at a bank in Fairbanks. I have to train employees in the new system."

"I wish I understood computers better. I just know the rudiments to get by."

"I'll be glad to show you more," he offered eagerly. "I have a laptop. Maybe tonight when I get back I could give you a lesson on everything mine can do."

On the surface, his offer seemed sincere, but Clay understood the guy-on-the-make tone underneath. He knew exactly what was on Tim Bennett's mind and it had nothing to do with computers.

"Are you sure you won't be tired after working all day?" Gina asked considerately.

"Not at all. It's a date then?"

After a beat of hesitation, she suggested, "Why don't we meet in the parlor around eight."

"Parlor?" Tim looked disappointed, and Clay couldn't help a self-satisfied smile.

"Yes. We should be comfortable there. I'll make sure we have hot chocolate and cookies to go with the computer lessons."

Recovering quickly, Tim agreed. "That sounds good. I'll see you tonight then."

After the door swung shut behind the guest, Clay glanced at Gina. "You really want to learn about computers with him?" The thought rankled, and Clay couldn't believe how uncomfortable he felt with the idea of her and Tim having a confab in the parlor.

"He's a guest, Clay. I'm just trying to be polite. Besides, it would be fun learning a few things. The program you use for billing is easy, but I wouldn't mind getting beyond that."

Clay couldn't get the picture out of his head of Gina and Bennett sitting on the sofa shoulder to shoulder, thigh to thigh with a laptop between them. Suddenly he was filled with the desire to spend time with her…not to convince her to marry him, he told himself, but to assure himself they were compatible.

"You said all the guests are leaving on Sunday?"

"That's right. No one's booked a room for next week."

"Monday morning I have to take medical supplies to a small village up north. How would you like to go along? It will be an overnight trip. It can give you a taste of flying and a different side of Alaskan life.''

Bringing the bowl of eggs to the stove, she poured them into the frying pan, set the bowl down, and looked up at him. "Where would we stay?"

If she was expecting a four-star hotel, he might as well disillusion her now. "I stay with a doctor who runs the clinic. He has a spare room with two cots."

"We'd be sleeping in the same room?"

"If we get married, we'll be sleeping in the same *bed*."

Her gaze locked to his and he could envision her on his sheets, underneath him. Blanking the vision from his mind, he assured her, "You can trust me, Gina. I won't make a move on you. At least not until you make up your mind," he said with a grin that he hoped would lighten the atmosphere between them.

She returned his smile with a small one of her own that told him she was taking everything about his proposal seriously. "I trust you, Clay. I just wasn't sure how it would look…if people would talk if we sleep in the same room together."

He laughed. "You're not in San Francisco now. Life up here is beyond gossip. We do what's necessary when it's necessary. Male…female…doesn't enter into it. Believe me, no one in Deep River will think twice about us sleeping in Jed's spare room."

Gina squared her shoulders and turned on the burner under the eggs. "Then I'll go with you. I came to Alaska for adventure and this sounds like one."

Clay was glad Gina had agreed to go along, but her words troubled him. She thought the trip would be an adventure…to him it was his everyday life.

Chapter Three

The twin engine plane soared over landscape covered with snow as Clay flew northeast. Gina had never seen land like this...untouched by human hands. Alaska was still the last great frontier, especially this part of it. They were headed toward Deep River, a village along the Yukon River.

Gina had been both excited and anxious about this trip. She was glad for it, glad she'd spend more time with Clay and get to know him better. That would make her decision easier. On the other hand, he would get to know her, too. What if he decided the chemistry wasn't enough? What if he decided she wouldn't fit into his life?

"Are you all right?" Clay spoke into his headset and glanced over at her.

Headsets made it possible to talk over the noise of the engines. "I'm fine. It's absolutely beautiful up here. No wonder you love flying."

He grinned at her, and she could see that nothing on this earth pleasured him more.

"How many people live in Deep River?" she asked.

"Ninety-eight at last count. That was six months ago. But Jack Kuzinsky who bought the trading post from my grandfather might have become a father by now. His wife was expecting."

"With only a hundred residents...does the town have a hospital?"

Clay smiled, and Gina knew the question must have sounded foolish. "No hospital," he answered. "A clinic with a doctor and a nurse. By clinic, I don't mean anything fancy. There are no roads to Deep River. Supplies come in mostly by plane."

"Did you say your grandfather lived in Deep River?"

"Yep. That's where Dad was born. He migrated to Fairbanks when he was twenty, doing odd jobs until he found work with a man who owned a leather shop. The owner's family apparently struck it rich during the gold rush. He had his own plane, and that's when Dad got interested in flying."

As Clay circled an area where birch and spruce were abundant, he pointed out the outline of the village and the airstrip where they'd be landing. Five minutes later, Gina was holding her breath as the wheels of the plane touched down. Clay taxied close to an outbuilding then cut the engine. After Clay helped Gina open the door next to her, she climbed up onto the wing. He watched as she jumped down without hesitating. When he landed beside her, he gazed down at her and her thoughts scattered.

She stepped back and her new boots felt stiff. Clay

had taken her to town on Saturday and advised her on what she'd need to come on this trip. She'd bought long underwear, a combination hiking and snow boot, a fur-lined cap with earflaps, and an insulated vest for under her parka. He'd insisted she'd need it all eventually if she was going to spend the winter in Alaska. She couldn't imagine how she'd look with earflaps down on that cap and wasn't about to do it for Clay to see.

"Where's your hat?" he asked, as if he'd read her thoughts.

"In my duffel."

"You're going to need it. We're walking everywhere we go."

"It seems colder here than in Fairbanks."

"About ten degrees colder. Do you want to wait in the shed while I tie down the plane and unload the supplies?"

"I'm fine."

His still intent look told her he'd be watching her carefully during this trip. Maybe his scrutiny would make her feel less attracted to him, less eager to feel his arms around her again. Yet she doubted that as she stood on the ground beside him, snow and firs, blue sky and crystal air surrounding them.

When she looked up at him, she was struck again by how tall he was...at least six-one. He seemed even taller in these surroundings. His brown suede, lambswool-lined parka fit him comfortably, and the hood emphasized the width of his shoulders. His brown hair blew in a sudden gust of wind.

He belonged here.

Turning away from her at last, Clay made quick work of securing the plane and stacking supplies on a sled that looked more like a wagon. Then he picked up both their bags, put them on top and nodded toward a trail. "Come on. It's about half a mile to Jed's cabin."

Their breath formed ribbons of white vapor as they walked, and Clay pulled the sled behind them. Gina absorbed the untamed nature of the land, the unmarked trail Clay seemed to know by instinct.

When they arrived at the cabin where they'd be staying, Gina saw it was a *real* cabin, not a log home or a prefabricated getaway...an honest-to-goodness wood cabin. The door was unlocked and Clay opened it. "Go on in," he told her.

The inside wasn't warm, though. A wood stove stood to one side of the room.

"Is there heat?" she asked Clay.

He went to the sled and removed one of the boxes, bringing it inside. "The cabin was modernized before Jed moved up here. It has oil heat...running water, too. And a real bathroom. But when Jed's not here, he doesn't waste fuel or wood."

As Clay smiled at her, she felt like an idiot. "I'm sorry. I didn't know what to expect."

He shrugged. "This is a different life than the one you're used to. Do you want to stay here and warm up while I take the supplies to the clinic? It's another good half mile. I can get a fire going in the stove."

The walk had energized her, not tired her out. "I'm fit, Clay. I do yoga every morning and aerobics three or four times a week. In college I ran track. My stamina might not be *that* good anymore, but a hike here or there isn't going to wear me out."

If he was surprised by her words, he didn't show

it. "I'm glad to hear it. You'll enjoy this trip more if you get to meet everybody and see everything."

Gina tried to absorb everything around her as they set out again—houses that were grouped close together, a generator shed, a cemetery. The half mile seemed to pass in a flash as they neared the center of the village and two dogs ran by her. The community was more or less arranged around a clinic, the Trading Post, the school and the church. Everyone they passed knew Clay.

When they reached the clinic, Jed and the nurse there greeted him like a long lost friend.

Jed's black eyebrows raised when he spotted Gina, and he glanced at his friend.

Forestalling questions, Clay explained, "This is Gina Foster, our..." He corrected himself, "My lodge manager. I offered to bring her along to show her a different side of Alaska."

Jed smiled engagingly and Gina wondered how many hearts he'd broken with his dark good looks and deep green eyes. "No man's land, he means," Jed commented with a wink. "Life here isn't for the weak-hearted."

"Don't listen to a word he says," the pretty blond nurse interjected. "I'm Nancy Belkins." She extended her hand to Gina. "We're quite civilized, probably friendlier than most because we have to pull together. I don't know what we'd do without adventurers like Clay. There aren't many of them around anymore."

"I'm not an adventurer," Clay protested with a crooked smile. "I'm a pilot."

"Same difference," Nancy teased.

Already, Gina knew she'd fallen hard for Clay Mc-

Cormick. But at that moment, as she was beguiled by his irresistible grin, his explorer spirit, his straight-arrow honesty, she realized marriage to him would be unpredictable, exciting and always an adventure. Could she handle that? What if he decided to leave Fairbanks and live in a place like this? Men like him did that.

She was insecure about her own ability to handle life. After all, she hadn't had much practice on her own. Clay was so confident, so self assured, so… much a man. All those years under her father's protective care were hard to slough off, but she was trying. She just wanted to make sure she made the right decisions while she did it. If she married Clay Mc-Cormick, that would be the biggest decision of her life.

Jed offered to take Clay and Gina to lunch at the Trading Post down the street—if the earth-packed, snow rutted thoroughfare could be called that. Gina had seen three-and four-wheel all-terrain vehicles on their walk to the village and realized that's how most people got around.

As Jed, Gina and Clay walked down the street, she spotted a shiny red pickup truck and asked both men, "How do you get vehicles here when there aren't any roads?"

Jed answered her, "Freight planes. That little beauty was delivered by Sky Van about a week ago. It's Fred Olan's and he's pleased as punch to have it. I think he's given everyone in town a ride in it."

Clay chuckled. "He's wanted a pickup like that for the past ten years. What made him buy it now?"

"He said he's getting too old to save his money and he might as well use it up while he can."

As they walked and talked, Gina could sense a real camaraderie between Jed and Clay, and she wondered how long they'd known each other.

Lunch at the Trading Post consisted of hamburgers—the selection for the day. The owner of the Trading Post, Jack Kuzinsky, fried them while Clay pulled out a chair for Gina at one of the two tables sandwiched in among the dry goods and supplies.

Gina listened to the conversation between Clay and Jed, learning more about Deep River. She discovered that the air strip they had landed on was maintained by the state, or at least by state funds. One of the villagers ran the grader and had the responsibility for maintaining the air strip.

Seeing Gina's interest in the subject, Jed said to Clay, "Tell her what you use as a barometer to land your plane when the runway's icy."

Clay frowned for a moment as if the telling might not be a good idea.

"Tell me," Gina insisted.

"A couple of the villagers have four wheel drive vehicles. When the runway's icy, one of them drives down the runway, picks up as much speed as he can and then brakes. When I radio in, he tells me the distance it took to stop."

"Isn't that risky?"

"Whoever does it knows what he's doing and so do I. Sometimes the flight can't wait. Today's batch of supplies was just a usual monthly order, but other times a particular medication might be needed." Clay turned to Jed, "Have you seen Ben lately?"

"Not since I gave him that medicine for his arthritis a month ago. You know him. He sticks to himself."

"Yeah, I know. I brought him some of that apricot tobacco he likes." Then he explained to Gina, "Ben Attala knew my grandfather and my dad. His mother was of Athabascan descent and for years he strictly adhered to the old ways. He trapped and fished and lived off the land. He still does to a certain extent, but he's modernizing some, too. I'd like to take that tobacco over to him this afternoon so I can get back before dark. Are you interested in coming along or have you done enough hiking for one day? His place is about a mile north of town."

Amazingly, Gina felt wonderful. She was probably on an adrenaline rush. She wanted to see and do everything she could, as well as be with Clay as much as possible. "I'd like to go with you." She motioned to the back of the Trading Post. "I'm going to freshen up first. It will only take me five minutes."

Clay watched Gina as she walked between tables to the rear of the store. Her jeans were snug and showed off her curves. She'd taken off her vest. Her sweater, which looked like cashmere, came to her waist and was a bit loose and swung as she walked. The soft material delineated her breasts, and Clay felt the desire stir that was so much a part of him whenever she was around.

"Cute," Jed commented. "Here I thought you'd hired a fifty-year-old battle-ax for your lodge manager. She's awfully young, isn't she?"

"Twenty-three. She was affordable. Believe it or not, she did have some experience. I'm thinking about marrying her."

With that, Jed's head jerked up. "Do you want to explain that?"

He and Jed had been friends the past two years,

ever since Jed had taken the position here at Deep River. Now Clay told him about his father's will and the stipulation that he marry.

"What happens after the year?" Jed asked.

"I don't know. I guess we'll just have to wait and see. That's if she agrees to marry me."

Jed's green eyes were serious as he advised, "You could be tying yourself in a knot that won't be so easy to untangle."

Clay knew Jed had taken this post in Deep River to escape his own tangled past. "After Elizabeth left, I vowed I'd never marry again. But Dad's left me no choice. If Gina and I know the terms and the stakes going in, we'll keep it simple."

"Marriage is *never* simple," Jed insisted.

Because Gina returned to the table then, Clay didn't have the opportunity to comment.

She smiled at them both. "I'm ready whenever you are."

Her smile did crazy things to Clay's libido. He wanted to ask her for her answer to his proposal right now so he could stop wondering and thinking about what they might be like together. But he'd told her he'd give her a week and he would.

Fifteen minutes later, Clay and Gina walked side by side in the bright sunlight. The snow had melted in patches and she was watching her step so she didn't slip. When the street ended, he motioned to a trail through the spruce. "It's this way. Close to the river."

Clay shortened his stride so Gina wouldn't have trouble keeping up with him. She'd finally put down the earflaps on her hat. She looked adorable...and she was so much younger than he was. Eleven years. Did age matter? Was he taking unfair advantage of her?

"Tell me why you left San Francisco," he requested casually as they walked.

Her gaze swung up to his and he saw reluctance there. "It's a long story."

"We have half a mile yet, so I have time." He hoped he could put her at ease.

After she glanced at him again, she gave in to his request. "My dad has always thought he knows exactly what I should do and how I should do it."

"Parents are like that."

"Maybe. But my father's very forceful."

"You said your mom died when you were seven?"

"Yes. My father hired a full-time nanny, Miss Bloomfield. When my mom was alive, I was with the housekeeper in the evenings. My dad's business required that he and my mother go out a lot together. I was used to that and I liked Hildy. But after my mom died, she left. Dad never would tell me why, but I think she just didn't like him. She considered herself working for mom and when my mother wasn't around anymore, she didn't want to stay."

"So was Miss Bloomfield tall and thin with a bun on top of her head?"

"She was short and *round* with a bun on top of her head." Gina glanced at Clay and they both laughed.

He couldn't remember the last time he'd laughed with a woman like that. "What happened when she left?"

"Dad hired someone else. Neither was as warm as Hildy. Both of them were just doing a job, and I was lonely a lot. My father sent me to an all-girl's school that was as strict as he was, so I learned to toe the line early. I learned what was expected of me. I learned not to make waves.''

"You didn't rebel as a teenager?''

"I guess I was too busy to rebel, or didn't know I should. I was in boarding school then and wanted to make my father proud of me. I put a lot of time into my studies. On the weekends, I volunteered at the hospital for something to do.''

"And college?''

"I guess you could say I didn't really know how to have fun. I went to an all-women's college. It suited me. Some of the girls would come back with stories of visiting nearby colleges, going to fraternity parties, getting drunk. That just wasn't my thing.''

"Didn't it all change when you graduated and found a job?''

"I guess it could have. It should have. But I hadn't seen much of my dad in all those years between boarding school and college. I longed to have some kind of connection to him.'' Their boots crunched in the snow as they hiked. Clay noticed that there were other sets of tracks, probably Ben's, but he was more intent on Gina's story than figuring out how many times Ben had come and gone in the past day or so.

"What sparked your leaving San Francisco?'' After the sheltered life she'd led, something must have.

Gina's cheeks were rosy from the cold, but he could swear they got even redder. "I started dating a man who worked for my father. He wanted to get serious a lot faster than I did.''

"Did your father approve?''

"That was the problem. He wanted me to marry Trent.''

"But you weren't ready for marriage?''

"It's a little more complicated than that, but I wanted to make my own decision in my own time. I felt I wouldn't be able to if I stayed."

"Does your dad know where you are?"

"I left him a note telling him not to worry, and another letter after I took the job at the lodge. Then I wrote to him a few months after that to give him my actual location. He flew up, and we saw each other in Fairbanks in July."

Clay had a feeling there was a lot she wasn't saying.

"He wanted to take me home," she finally went on. "I told him I wasn't going with him."

"And he gave up?"

"My father never gives up. Every time I talk with him he tries to convince me to come home. At least for now, he's accepted the idea that I'm here for a while."

For a while, Clay repeated to himself. Alaska wasn't in Gina's blood, and he doubted if it ever would be.

A short while later, they reached a cabin that looked much like Jed's, only it was smaller. There was a snow machine parked along the side.

Gina motioned to it. "I guess there are ways to get around other than cars."

"Ben has a canoe for the river in summer, too." Clay knocked on the door.

A few moments later, Ben opened it.

"Clay!" He greeted his friend with a wide smile. Then he frowned. "I'm so sorry to hear about your father. I missed him after he moved to Fairbanks. The past ten years we didn't see each other as much as we should have."

Clay spent enough time alone with his grief in the dark of night. He didn't want to discuss it now.

Changing the subject, he glanced at Gina. "I brought someone to meet you. Gina Foster, Ben Attala." Clay could see her studying Ben as she shook hands with him. His hair was gray and he wore it long, tied with a leather thong at his neck. His eyebrows were heavy, his forehead high. His cheekbones and the structure of his face spoke of his Athabascan heritage.

"Welcome, Gina," the older man said heartily. "John wrote to me about you. He told me you relieved a great burden from his shoulders. He didn't have to worry about the lodge after you came."

Clay saw Gina's eyes become moist. "Thank you for telling me that."

"Come on in," Ben said enthusiastically.

The inside of Ben's cabin was much different than Jed's. There was a colorful wool blanket hanging on one wall, rag rugs on the plank floor, a wolverine pelt on another wall while a wood stove warmed the interior of the cabin.

Ben motioned to a sitting area where a cane rocker stood across from a hand-carved sofa with leather cushions. Clay knew Ben had crafted all of it himself.

Before he joined Gina on the sofa, Clay handed Ben the pouch of tobacco.

A smile lit the old man's features. "You never forget."

"Small pleasures are important ones," Clay said, and Ben nodded his agreement.

From what Gina had told him, Clay realized she'd led a quiet reserved life, not spending a lot of time socializing. Over the past few months, he'd noticed she had no problem relating to anyone. When she spoke with Ben now, Clay understood why. She truly knew how to listen and put whoever she was speaking to at the center of her world. At that particular moment, it made awkwardness vanish and conversation flow. Because of her questions and her interest, she pulled tales from Ben that Clay had not even heard concerning the history of the area, stories of ice breaking early and floods, Ben's travels on the river when he was a young man.

The time passed quickly until Clay checked his watch. "We'd better be getting back to Jed's. He's actually planning to cook for us tonight."

Ben frowned. "That boy does a lot of good here, but he's a lone wolf who walks on the outside."

While they'd talked, they'd sipped tea and snacked on a biscuit type of cookie that Ben had baked and kept in a tin for the occasional visitor.

As Gina rose with Clay, she said, "Thank you for your hospitality. I really enjoyed this."

"You're welcome to come back again anytime Clay flies up here."

When Clay helped Gina with her jacket, he couldn't help lifting her hair over her collar. She glanced up at him over her shoulder and their gazes met. An electrifying zing was still there, and the time they'd spent together today had added to its intensity.

Ben cleared his throat. "Are you flying out tomorrow?"

Clay concentrated on Ben's question with difficulty. "Yes. Anything in particular you want me to bring on the next trip up?"

Ben shook his head. "I have everything I need."

Clay smiled and shook the older man's hand.

As they began the walk back to Jed's cabin, neither Clay nor Gina spoke. Clay wondered if Ben's stories of the wilderness had frightened her, if she was thinking about the ice breaking and the river flooding, and wind chills fifty-eight degrees below zero. Maybe it had been a mistake to bring her here. After all, life at the lodge was pretty civilized. Still, he wondered how long it would be until she would miss the conveniences she'd left, a place where she'd lived all her life, a climate that was kinder.

They were still a half mile from town when light began to fade and Clay led Gina on the trail through spruce that had stood for decades in testament to the elements. Gina's steps were slower now and she looked as if she were beginning to tire. She'd done remarkably well today.

Clay was so caught up in studying her, thoughts about what might or might not happen between them, that he'd forgotten one of the first rules of survival in this almost-primitive land—make noise while you're hiking. He heard the rustle of boughs, the breaking of a branch. The sounds didn't register as they should have because he was intent on Gina.

Suddenly there was a shadow and then a noise, not quite a growl. A six-foot bear rose up on the trail before them.

Clay caught Gina's arm just as she saw the animal and exclaimed, "Oh my gosh!"

"Don't move," he said in a low voice, knowing her first instinct might be to run. Black bears usually didn't go out of their way to attack humans. It was pretty much live and let live unless you got too close to their cubs.

Clay glanced at Gina and saw she was panicked. Her face was white, and she looked deathly afraid.

Staring at the bear, Clay tried to get a sense of how much danger they were in. This fellow was probably doing the last few days of foraging before he hibernated for the winter. Thank goodness they were downwind.

The bear raised his head, sniffed into the air and came down again on all fours with a last look at them. Then he ambled off.

Clay heaved a sigh of relief. His hand was on Gina's arm and she still stood frozen. "It's all right," he said. "He's gone."

She turned to him then, eyes still wide, her face pale. He could see her lower lip quiver.

"It's all right," he reassured her again, closing her into his arms.

Hunched against his chest, she whispered, "We could have been killed."

"Most black bears aren't aggressive. We should have been making noise to let him know we were coming through. He would have stayed away then."

"You can't know that. He might have come after us."

Taking Gina by the shoulders, Clay looked down into her eyes. "There are certain rules out here, Gina. I shouldn't have been so blasé about bringing you here. Even *I* forgot them while we were walking. This is what Alaska is all about, even the civilized parts. You have to expect the unexpected. You have to be prepared. This is the life you'd accept if you marry me."

When she gazed up at him, he saw the doubts there,

all the questions, and confusion, too. Was her financial independence worth facing the unpredictable and dealing with the elements...as well as marrying a stranger?

Chapter Four

When it came time to turn in that night, Gina followed Clay into Jed's spare bedroom. She felt self-conscious and awkward. Meeting a bear for the first time didn't seem as dangerous as sleeping in the same room with Clay.

This afternoon she'd realized so many things. She'd discovered a whole new world with Clay. It might have its bears and unblazed trails, but when Clay had taken her into his arms, she'd felt safe. He was a protective man, a proud man, an adventurous man, and obviously he had doubts about her fitting into his life. She hadn't coped very well with the bear.

They crossed to the cot where he'd placed his duffel bag. "Do you want me to sleep out in the living room? I can bed down on the floor."

"The floor's cold and hard," she reminded him.

"For the past fifteen minutes, you've been jittery and can't even meet my eyes. If you don't trust me, if that's all about sleeping in here together—"

"I've never slept in the same room with a man before. I don't know how I'm supposed to act."

He'd been about to unzip his duffel, but now he straightened. "You've never slept in the same room with a man before?"

Part of her explanation for her jitters had just slipped out. "No, I haven't."

He was staring at her intently now, and she felt like a butterfly pinned to a board.

"What?" she asked, a bit defiantly.

"I want to make sure I understand this. You've never had a man as a roommate before? Or you've never *slept* with a man before?"

"I've never done either," she said quickly, to do away with the subject once and for all.

He looked amazed. "What about this guy you've been dating? I thought he wanted to marry you."

Trent obviously hadn't wanted to marry her because of her seduction skills. "We hadn't gotten that far. I wasn't that serious."

"So you're still a virgin?"

Taking a deep breath, she expelled it with her answer. "Yes."

He seemed to take that admission like a blow. Swearing, he snatched up his duffel. "I'm sleeping in the living room."

Impulsively she caught his arm, realizing she wanted intimacy with Clay...even the simple intimacy of sleeping in the same room in different beds. She wanted to see what it felt like. She was so curious about her feelings about him, how they'd be together, what he'd look like while he was asleep.

"I may be a virgin, Clay, but I'm not a child. I'm

twenty-three and it's about time I got over my shyness. We're friends, aren't we?"

He didn't look convinced, but he answered, "We're on that road."

"Then let's not make this a big deal."

The wind had picked up with the onset of night and it rattled the window, its chill seeping inside.

"I'll feel safer if you're in here with me," she added quietly.

His expression gentled. "I see. You'd like to have me around in case a bear tries to get in."

There was amusement in his voice, and she could tell he wasn't offended. "Exactly." She grinned at him. Then what he'd said sank in. "A bear wouldn't try to do that, would he?"

Clay laughed. "I think you've seen your last bear for this trip. You're safe here."

He hadn't answered her exactly, and she hoped he was right. She did know she was safe here. She was safe with *him*.

Still, after she'd changed and reentered the room, she wondered what Clay thought about her floor-length pink flannel nightgown with ruffled cuffs and ruffle around the collar. His penetrating gaze on her as she crossed to her cot made her tremble. He was lying on his mattress, dressed in gray sweats, his arm thrown behind his head as he reclined on two pillows. That electric tension zipped between them again.

"Should I turn off the light?" she asked.

He nodded.

After she switched off the lamp, she settled onto her cot with the covers pulled to her chin. She could still feel Clay's gaze on her in the dark room and wondered if his imagination was conjuring up erotic images as hers was. Just the thought of him kissing her again caused her to push down the covers.

In the darkness, questions she'd been holding at bay became too loud to ignore. What if she married Clay and he decided he hated being married to her? What if she wasn't enough woman for him? What if he wanted someone more experienced...not only with men, but with life here?

His voice was deep and husky in the darkness, "Good night, Gina."

He seemed very close, yet very far away. "'Night, Clay."

She knew she wouldn't be dreaming of bears tonight, but of Clay and the decision she had to make.

There was a luxury sedan parked at the side entrance of the lodge when Clay and Gina returned. "I thought you said we didn't have any bookings this week," Clay commented.

"We don't. Unless someone just decided to stop to see if we have vacancies. Murray must have let them inside."

Murray was the caretaker and all-around handyman. He was getting up in years, but John McCormick had kept him on because he trusted him. In his sixties, Murray still split firewood with the best of them.

Clay parked beside the sleek black Lexus. Gina didn't wait for him to open the door, but hopped out and hurried up the walk to the lodge. As soon as she opened the side door, she heard voices. She froze as she recognized the loudest one, experiencing almost the same kind of panic she'd felt coming face-to-face with the bear. Standing perfectly still, she hadn't moved when Clay came in behind her.

"What's wrong?" he asked.

"It's my father," she said in a low voice. "I hear him."

Clay clasped her shoulder as if he was remembering everything she'd told him about Wesley Foster. "Why don't we go see what he wants."

"I know what he wants, and I'm not going back."

"Come on," Clay urged, nudging her forward. "Maybe he just came for a visit."

She prayed Clay was right but knew deep in her soul that he wasn't.

Removing her parka, she laid it on the bench in the hallway and squared her shoulders. She had to keep her wits about her.

Clay tossed his jacket onto the bench, too. As they neared the sitting room, he said, "I hear two voices, and one of them isn't Murray's."

When Gina reached the doorway, she received her second surprise. Trent Jones was with her father and he was smiling at her.

"Well, there you are!" Wesley Foster boomed. "The caretaker said you were off in some village somewhere. In a small plane at that. Have you lost your mind?"

"It's good to see you, too, Dad." Her voice was wry.

"Your father was worried and so was I," Trent said, coming forward now.

"There was no reason for either of you to be worried. Clay's an excellent pilot. I enjoyed the village very much. I even saw a bear." She said it with some pride and saw Clay's frown. She'd been scared out of her wits, but her father didn't need to know that.

"That's it," Wesley said, throwing his hands up in the air. "Trent and I came to take you home before winter sets in. Believe me, you won't want to be here."

"I'm not going home, Dad. Let's get that straight right now. I'd like you to meet Clay McCormick. He owns the lodge and his own flying service."

Her father reluctantly shook Clay's hand. "Your caretaker said you don't have any guests. If your business is this bad now, what happens in the winter?"

"Alaskans are used to winter, Mr. Foster," Clay answered with a forced smile. "Our tourist season might slow, but we still have businessmen who come to Fairbanks. We also have winter enthusiasts. While there's a lull, I take the time to make renovations and changes in the lodge."

"You intend to keep paying Gina the same salary even though it's only half the work?"

"It's not half the work. It's different work. Instead of catering to guests, she'll be housecleaning, developing menus, creating our spring ads."

"So she'll be a glorified cleaning lady," Wesley mused.

Gina always knew her father could be frustrating. Now he was at his finest. "How long will you be staying?"

"As long as it takes to convince you to return home. I brought a few things to help you remember what San Francisco's like—fresh raspberry pie, Chinese take-out from the Green Dragon." From his pocket, he drew out a silk scarf. "From that little boutique you like so much. And I have something even more special that I'll give you later tonight.''

"You haven't told me how long you're staying.'' He'd brought favorite foods and the design on the scarf was lovely. But he wasn't simply being thoughtful. He was trying to bribe her.

"A few days. Obviously you have room. I'm sure Mr. McCormick doesn't want to turn away two paying customers.''

"Is your luggage still in the car?'' Clay asked tersely, his jaw set.

"Yes,'' Trent answered. "Your Mr. Murray said to leave it there until we made arrangements with you. I suppose he wanted to verify who we were.''

"It's not *Mr.* Murray,'' Gina told Trent. "The first name is Murray. He doesn't stand on formality. Most people don't up here.''

Trent and Wesley Foster exchanged a look.

Before they caught her up in another conversation, she took the offensive. "Since we didn't expect guests, I don't have dinner planned. How does Fettuccini Alfredo sound?''

"Wonderful,'' Trent decided. "Especially if you're cooking it. I know how good you are.''

With that, she caught a glimpse of Clay frowning. Actually it was more like a scowl.

Trent went on, "I brought a bottle of the best California Chardonnay. It will go wonderfully with pasta. So will the raspberry pie,'' he added with a wink. "Oh, and I think your dad forgot to tell you—we brought fresh pineapple, too.''

They were tempting her with her favorite treats, but none of it would entice her away from her job—or Clay.

While Clay started a fire in the hearth in the sitting room, Gina went to the kitchen to prepare dinner.

She was making the sauce for the fettuccini when Clay entered the kitchen. "Do you need help?" he asked.

"Do you evict unwanted guests?"

At that he smiled. "They *are* a pair. I brought their luggage in. I didn't know which rooms you wanted to assign to them. Are you going to give your dad one of the suites?"

She shook her head. "I don't want him up on my floor brow-beating me."

Moving closer to her, Clay clasped her shoulder. "I think you've held your own up to now if that's any consolation."

Her heart always raced when Clay was near to her like this...when they were within touching distance. Concentrating on their conversation, she thought about Clay's comment. Actually, she *was* proud of herself. Though her father's approval still meant a lot to her, it didn't mean the world anymore. She had to find her own way, not accept his. Maybe she'd made some strides after all.

She gazed up at Clay, and her father and Trent seemed far away. "Thanks for your support."

Brushing her hair behind her ear, he said roughly, "Anytime." Then clearing his throat, he stepped away. "The water for the pasta is boiling."

She wished he'd kiss her again. She wished her father and Trent were back in San Francisco.

Clay helped Gina put dinner on the table, and she saw Trent eyeing him warily. She'd always thought Trent was a handsome man, but there was no comparison to Clay. Trent was a stepped-from-a-magazine kind of handsome. Clay on the other hand had a rugged face, and his chiseled jawline added to his attractiveness…as did his shaggy hair. Trent's too-perfectly groomed blond hair, designer shirt and trousers—though casual—made him look out of place here.

Throughout dinner, Trent monopolized Gina as best he could, leaving Clay to deal with her father. She heard her dad bragging about his new trade agreements to sell his electronic parts in China. She also heard him explaining how Trent had risen in the ranks of his company and now he was invaluable. That didn't surprise Gina, and she couldn't help but wonder if Trent's value might have more to do with his success in persuading her to leave Alaska.

"The village actually had no roads?" Trent asked her, in keeping with their conversation.

"No *paved* roads," she corrected him. "It's beautiful country. You should see it sometime."

"I've always wanted to take a cruise up this way. I've just never had the time."

Gina knew seeing Alaska's beautiful sights from a cruise ship was a far cry from actually living the experience.

After a short pause, Trent clasped her hand. "I'd like to talk to you privately after dinner."

Slowly she extricated her hand from under Trent's. She felt nothing when he touched her compared to the scorching awareness whenever Clay's skin brushed hers. "I was going to spend some time with Dad and then I need to turn in. I have an early day tomorrow." She had housekeeping chores to get ready for next week's guests. She also wanted to call Mary Lou and pay Bobby a visit to read him the story she'd promised him.

"You can't avoid me forever, Gina. We have to talk about the way you left."

"I left because I felt I had no choice," she said quietly.

Just then Wesley addressed her. "How about some of that raspberry pie? Everything's great, Gina. You've turned into a fine little cook."

"I've known how to cook since boarding school, Dad. I guess you just never had a chance to sample what I made before."

Wesley Foster stared at her, studying her as if realizing he didn't know her at all. It made her sad that he didn't. He didn't know how she'd always longed to have a close relationship with him, how lonely she'd been after her mother died, how isolated she'd felt at boarding school. They'd spent all of their holidays together, a ritual that had led her to believe he cared about her and was willing to make time for her...at least on those days. But the rest of the year, his brief phone calls seemed more duty than anything else.

Yet the past was the past. All she could do was move forward and hope they could get to know each other again now.

"I'll get that pie," she said softly, rising to her feet, knowing it would be the best raspberry pie she'd ever tasted. That's what her father intended.

Conversation didn't flow easily with dessert and coffee. Clay became more and more remote. Maybe that was because her father kept referring to their circle of friends in San Francisco, reminding her how everyone missed her, teasing her with the cultural events she'd missed, all in all putting forth his case why she should return with him without actually saying it.

After they finished with coffee, Clay offered to take the luggage to the men's rooms. As he exited the dining room, Gina knew he probably wanted to return to his house. He hadn't been home since yesterday morning. She wondered if he thought of his house as a home—a refuge. She'd never been inside. She wished she knew what Clay was thinking...about her reaction to the run-in with the bear...about sleeping in the same room together.

Had he dreamt of her the way she'd dreamt of him?

As Clay took Trent Jones and Wesley Foster to their rooms, he decided Foster was a pompous ass and Jones not much more than a puppet. Had Gina actually considered marrying the man? She'd dated him. Though she'd admitted she hadn't been ready for a serious relationship, she must have had feelings for him. The way they'd been locked in conversation tonight, maybe she'd missed him. Maybe she missed everything about her life in San Francisco. Maybe her father's trip up here had accomplished exactly what he'd planned.

After Clay returned downstairs, he decided to bring in firewood. If Gina needed it tomorrow, she'd have plenty. He filled the storage bin beside the fireplace along with the carrier on the hearth, then went to the office and switched on the computer. He checked on the weather for the next day, then called his client— a businessman he was supposed to fly to Anchorage. He could have done all of this at his house, but he felt the need to talk with Gina and spend a few more minutes with her alone before he left. Maybe he just wanted to see if Wesley Foster's temptations and persuasive arguments had convinced her to go back to San Francisco with him.

After Clay called his client, he dialed Dave to see if anything had come up at the hangar he needed to take care of. It was almost an hour later when he finished and decided to find Gina. He didn't trust Jones, and he didn't want the man cornering her.

When Clay exited the office, he heard voices in the parlor and headed that way. He stopped in the doorway. The tableau before him clued him in that something important was happening. Jones was seated on the sofa next to Gina. She was turned almost sideways, her knees grazing his.

Her father stood above her, clasping something around her neck. "This ruby necklace was your mother's favorite. I've been saving it until you were old enough to appreciate it."

Gina reverently fingered the ruby lavaliere. Not only was the pendant a ruby surrounded by smaller ones, there were gems glittering along the gold chain that Foster now fastened around her neck. It looked beautiful against her soft white sweater. It looked beautiful on her. Clay suspected Gina was used to this type of present, used to this kind of luxury. He'd noticed the gold charm bracelet she sometimes wore, the necklace with sapphires, the diamond stud earrings. All of it was second nature to her. If she married him, he couldn't afford those kind of luxuries on an ongoing basis. Why would she want to marry him? She could obviously have everything her heart desired back in San Francisco. He bet Foster even had a trust fund set up for her.

Although Gina touched the ruby necklace appreciating its beauty, loving the idea that it had been her mother's, she hated what her father and Trent had been trying to convince her to do for the past hour. Their trip here had been meant as an ambush. First Trent had apologized for rushing her the way he had. He'd said he was simply eager for them to start their lives together. Then her father had joined in encouraging them to think about a Christmas engagement. She'd told them both she didn't intend to get engaged at Christmas, that she had a different life now and needed to explore where she wanted it to take her, all the while thinking of Clay's proposal and what marrying him would mean.

That's when her father had pulled the necklace from his pocket and insisted on putting it around her neck. Sudden tears came to her eyes as she realized he never listened to her. Not really.

At that moment, she saw Clay standing in the doorway and felt relieved he hadn't left yet. She knew she had to make a decision now that would affect the rest of her life. She knew she had to be her own person...independent...separate from her father. She knew Trent Jones wasn't her future. Clay McCormick might be. There was only one way to find out. She had to take a risk and plunge into the unknown to find the happiness she was looking for.

Her gaze locked to Clay's, and her father's words faded away. With the necklace clasped around her neck, she stood, walked around the coffee table over to Clay and took his hand. "Dad, there's a very important reason why I can't come back to San Francisco with you, why I can't get engaged to Trent at Christmas." She glanced at Clay then looked at Trent, and finally her father. "I'm going to marry Clay."

Gina's words sank into Clay slowly. He felt a wash of amazement as well as relief flow through him as her gaze pleaded with him. He could see the fear in her eyes that he may have changed his mind about marriage...that he wouldn't go along with her on this.

She had just agreed to marry him!

If she did, he had no illusions about why she was doing it. Sheer rebellion. Her father had backed her into another corner. At this stage in her life, she'd decided she wouldn't let him do it. She saw marriage as a way out and that suited Clay just fine. He told himself the burst of joy inside of him *was* simply relief that his life would remain pretty much intact.

"I wondered when you were going to make the announcement," he said with a smile. "Now's the perfect time. Maybe your father can extend his stay a day or two and stay for the wedding."

"You're marrying *him?*" her father erupted. "Since when?"

"I've been here six months, Dad. It doesn't take that long to know someone's right for you."

"Right for you? He's a *pilot*. You're living in the middle of nowhere."

Trent looked shell-shocked.

"I'm sorry, Trent, that I didn't tell you right away," she apologized. "I thought you realized when I left that we weren't right for each other."

"You can't do this!" Trent suddenly exploded. "We should talk about it. And you certainly can't put a wedding together in a couple of days."

"A marriage license only takes twenty-four hours," Clay informed Jones. "We can go down to the Bureau of Vital Statistics and get it tomorrow morning. I know the minister of a church in Fairbanks. I'll phone him to check if he's free Thursday evening.''

"You two don't know what you're doing, getting married like this on the spur of the moment! You'll regret it,'' Foster protested.

"It might seem on the spur of the moment to you, Dad, but I've had time to think about it. This is what I want.''

For another few minutes, Gina fended off her father's intense protests. Finally he snapped, "Maybe you'll be more reasonable about this in the morning.''

Trent stopped and took a last long look at Gina as Foster left the sitting room. Clay didn't see disappointment in his gaze. It was something else—resentment maybe, pique and anger that he hadn't gotten what he wanted.

Gina just said again, "I'm sorry, Trent.''

"You'll live to regret this, Gina. You and I could have had everything together.''

Clay had a suspicion that Jones was speaking of Foster's wealth rather than Gina's happiness. With the two men gone, he turned to Gina. "Did you mean what you said? Or was it all a show for your father?''

Her blue eyes were guileless, her voice sincere. "I want to marry you, Clay. I want to help you keep the lodge.''

He knew her decision wasn't selfless. "And you want your freedom. The money I'm offering you can do that for you.''

She didn't deny it, but she added, "I want more than freedom. I want a different life than the one I had before. I think I can have that with you.''

At that moment, he felt so much older than she was, so much more world-worn. There was no innocence left in him. She was still filled to the brim with it. They were making a bargain for a year, and he didn't know if she would or could keep it. But they'd both try and maybe end up with having more than when they started. "You'll be ready to get married on Thursday?"

"I will be if you give me some time tomorrow to shop when we go into Fairbanks."

"Shop?"

She smiled at him. "I want to buy a wedding dress."

On Thursday evening, Gina's hands trembled as she fastened the button at the neck of her wedding dress. The reality of what she was doing had set in when her father had brought her to the church early so she could get ready. On the way to the church he'd glanced at her often, as if she'd lost her mind. Even after they'd entered the vestibule, he'd tried to persuade her to go home with him. But she'd made a decision and she was sticking by it, come hell or high blizzards. The moment her father had clasped the ruby necklace around her neck, Gina had realized she had to take the risk of marrying Clay to be happy. She'd fallen in love with him. She wanted to be with him. She wanted him to have his dreams.

What about your own dreams? a small voice inside her asked.

She was hoping she was within reaching distance of her dreams, too, as she dressed in the white crushed velvet, ankle-length dress, felt the softness of its white fur cuffs, the trim of white fur around her neck. She knew all of her dreams had to do with Clay and not much to do with the $50,000 he was offering her if she stayed married to him for a year. Somehow she would earn his love. Somehow she would show him that she could be exactly the wife he needed—not just for a year, but for a lifetime.

At the mirror, she pulled her hair away from her face and attached pearl barrettes on each side. All of her curls fell down the back of her head. She wanted to knock Clay's socks off and make him proud he was marrying her. After she'd told him she wanted to shop for a wedding dress, he'd insisted on arranging a small reception in the social hall attached to the church. He had a lot of friends, and he wanted her to meet them. First the suggestion had made her happy because she'd thought he was including her in his life. Then she'd realized he was probably doing it for her so her father didn't question this marriage, so her father would realize her life was here now and stop putting pressure on her. Clay was protective like that. She just wished he felt more than protectiveness. She wished he had feelings for her other than the desire she saw in his eyes.

Suddenly there was a knock on the door, and she opened it. Her father was standing there looking grim. "You can still call this off."

"I'm walking down that aisle, Dad, with or without you, and I'm going to marry Clay with or without your blessing."

A resigned look came over him then. After he studied her for a long time, he held his arm out to her. "You look more beautiful than I've ever seen you. You look so very much like your mother."

Nothing else her father could have said would have touched her more, and she felt tears come to her eyes. Giving him a tremulous smile, she hooked her hand into the crook of his elbow and they crossed the vestibule.

The small church was dimly lit for a candlelight ceremony. A sentinel of light flickered at every other pew. As the organ music played, Gina walked down the aisle with her father, gazing toward the altar and Clay. Greg was standing beside him as his best man, holding both of their rings for safekeeping since she didn't have any bridesmaids. She'd had no one to ask. She'd been so busy working the past six months, she hadn't taken time to make friends. Maybe that would change now. Maybe Clay's friends would become her friends.

Clay looked so handsome in his tux. As she walked toward him, as her dad formally gave her into Clay's keeping, Clay's eyes were fiery with the desire that she'd only glimpsed in the past.

The minister began with ''Dearly Beloved'' and Gina became caught up in the ceremony and emotion she'd never felt before. This was her wedding. The man beside her was going to be her husband. She told herself everything was all right. She told herself she was doing the right thing. She told herself she was doing the best thing.

When the time came to say her wedding vows, she said them from her heart. ''I, Gina, take thee, Clay, to have and to hold, for better for worse, for richer for poorer, in sickness and in health, as long as we both shall live.''

Then Clay gazed into her eyes, and she wasn't so sure what she saw in his. The desire had vanished. His expression was somber, his voice deep and without emotion as he made his promise. ''I, Clay, take thee Gina, to have and to hold, for better or worse, for richer for poorer, in sickness and in health, as long as we both shall live.''

She'd said her vows, he'd said his. She had just promised to love Clay forever.

Was this a forever-promise for Clay, too, or was he simply promising to stay married to her for a year?

Chapter Five

As Gina and Clay stood by a table with a three-tiered wedding cake, so many emotions bombarded Gina. Since the ceremony, Clay hadn't said two words to her. He'd stood beside her, introducing his friends who'd come through the receiving line. Then he'd placed his hand in the small of her back to guide her into the social hall. She was so aware of him she could hardly breathe. It had been that way before. Now they were married and he seemed bigger than life, more masculine than any man she'd ever come in contact with.

She had no idea what he was thinking or feeling about tonight or the rest of their marriage. He'd gone about preparing for this wedding very practically, as if he were preparing a flight plan or packing provisions to take to a remote village. For the past two days, she'd been telling herself she wasn't running away from her father, she was running toward Clay. Yet knowing he didn't have any feelings for her, knowing this was just a marriage of convenience, made all of her emotions seem foolish.

When Clay held out the cake knife to her, she took it. His hand, large and roughened, covered hers. They cut a slice, and using the knife, Clay deposited it on a dish.

He stood in front of her holding the plate, a crooked smile on his lips. "We're supposed to feed each other. Greg's standing over there with the camera waiting to take the picture."

Gina suddenly felt as if everything about this day was a sham—repeating vows that might not have a true meaning, posing for pictures in front of everyone as if they were really in love. She remembered Clay's kiss at the altar. It had been gentle and brief...yet deep. She'd responded completely to it, body and soul. She was in love with Clay. It was the first time she'd been in love with any man, and it was definitely a head-over-heels feeling. The question was—would Clay ever love her? Would he ever think of her as more than a means to an end?

Breaking off a piece of the cake, she held it to his lips. They were warm, and she could remember their feel, their taste, and their texture as he opened them and his tongue touched her fingertips. Her breath caught because she saw that light in his eyes that she'd have to deal with later tonight. She was looking forward to their wedding night, yet she was nervous, too. Maybe he could sense that.

His gaze on hers, he licked the icing from her fingers so sensually her toes almost curled. Then he said, "You look absolutely beautiful tonight."

She felt herself blush and wished she could prevent that. "Thank you."

When he fed her the cake, she sucked the cake crumbs from his finger, wordlessly telling him she wanted tonight, telling herself she could please him.

They mingled with their guests after that, nibbling from the light buffet, glancing at each other until Mary Lou drew Gina from her groom's side.

"I just wanted to tell you that when you get back to Clay's house, there's catered food waiting for you. Greg and I figured you'd appreciate that more than a toaster. There's also a bottle of champagne," she said with a wink. "I think wedding receptions are more for the guests than the bride and groom. You can have your own private celebration back home."

Tears came to Gina's eyes at Mary Lou and Greg's kindness. "It's so sweet of you."

"Not sweet, just practical. You two probably won't want to think about food for the next couple of days. Clay said you aren't going away now. Are you going to take a honeymoon later?"

Gina had no idea what later would bring. "I think we're just going to wait and see how things go— Clay's work, guests at the lodge."

"I'm glad Clay found someone to love," Mary Lou said gently. "His ex-wife did a real number on him."

"Divorce is always hard," Gina responded quietly, hoping Mary Lou would tell her more.

"I suppose. Elizabeth acted as if Clay was going to be her world. But she couldn't handle the long spells of darkness and the weather. Clay being gone as much as he is, too. I guess he's told you all about her."

Gina had to be truthful. "Actually, he hasn't."

After Mary Lou studied her for a moment, she said,

"Clay doesn't talk about himself easily. He might just want to leave the past in the past. It takes a while for trust to build in a marriage. You'll have years to get to know each other inside and out."

Gina realized that was exactly the kind of marriage she wanted. Did Clay?

Just then, Trent Jones materialized in front of her, his expression dark. "Can I talk to you?" He glanced at Mary Lou. "Privately?"

Knowing she had to finally confront Trent head-on, Gina explained to Mary Lou, "Trent is an old friend from San Francisco. He and my father are staying in a hotel near the airport tonight and leaving tomorrow."

"You go on," Mary Lou encouraged her. "I see Bobby has icing all over his face. By the way, he said you read stories better than anyone else."

Mary Lou's words warmed Gina's heart. After she and Clay had gotten their marriage license, she'd shopped for her wedding dress while Clay found a tux. Afterward, they'd stopped at Mary Lou and Greg's to invite them to the wedding, and Gina had taken the time to read Bobby the story she'd promised him.

As Mary Lou walked away, Trent took Gina's arm and ushered her toward a shadowed corner where a coatrack stood. He started right in. "Your marriage is a mistake, Gina, and you know it. I told you I would wait until you were ready."

The time had come for complete honesty. "I would never have been ready, Trent. I could never be ready to marry a man who wanted to marry me to further his career. I heard you and Dad talking. I know you made a deal with him—if you married me, you'd receive a promotion and bonus. What kind of marriage would we have had if you didn't even have any feelings for me? Nor I for you?''

Trent's jaw had clamped tight at her words and now he just studied her. "I'm sorry you heard that conversation. Is that why you left San Francisco?''

"That was one of the reasons. You and Dad were steamrolling me. He's done that all my life.''

For a few moments, Trent was silent. Then he protested, "We would have had a good marriage, Gina. You have breeding and a way with people. I could have given you anything your heart desires. We would have made a good couple...a successful couple.''

Maybe her head *was* in the clouds, but she wanted more than that. "That's not what I want from marriage, Trent. I want a partner who loves me and is committed to me for a lifetime. I want to grow old with somebody, not make social contacts and have lots of money. I'm not really what you needed.''

Trent almost scoffed. "You believe in fairy tales.'' He shook his head. "I don't think your father knows just how old-fashioned and unrealistic you are. He wanted a good match for you. I would have been that. If you think you're going to grow old with this McCormick, just wait until the Alaskan winter sets in. I think you'll return to San Francisco and realize what I have to offer is a lot more practical.''

When Gina sighed and looked over Trent's shoulder, realizing she'd never convince him, she saw Clay crossing to them. He had a determined expression on his face.

Clay had been watching Gina ever since Mary Lou whisked her away. He couldn't take his eyes off of her. That dress was simple, elegant and virginal. Yet it was seductive, too, in the way it hugged her body, the way it hinted at the woman beneath. He wasn't sure how to play tonight. He didn't want to push Gina or rush her or scare her. But he did *want* her.

Still, seeing her with Trent Jones now put a spanner in his thinking. Gina and her former boyfriend had been locked in intense conversation, and he wondered again if she still had feelings for the man. That wouldn't change just because she'd married Clay.

The point was—they *had* gotten married and he didn't like the way Jones looked at her.

Coming upon them, he circled his new bride's waist with his arm. "Are you ready to throw the bouquet and head back to the house?"

She looked up at him. "Yes. I was just saying goodbye to Trent."

Her voice was steady, but Clay saw that she looked upset and he wondered what kind of goodbye it had been. At least it wasn't a private one or more could have happened than a conversation. Was she having doubts about the marriage? Had she jumped in too impulsively?

"Let's go get your bouquet and we'll call it a night. Have a good flight back to San Francisco, Jones."

The man scowled as Clay guided Gina away from her old life into her new one.

Gina and Clay were in the car on the way to his house when he asked, "Are you having second thoughts about this marriage?"

She glanced over at him, "Why do you ask?"

"Because your conversation with Jones seemed pretty intense. I thought maybe you were wishing you were going back with him and picking up where you left off.''

There was a long moment of silence before she responded, ''I don't want to go back, Clay. Trent isn't the man I thought he was when I began dating him. I'm not having second thoughts. Are you?''

''No.'' He couldn't explain everything he was feeling, how much he was looking forward to tonight, along with her moving into his house. Maybe he'd simply been alone for too long.

After a few moments, Gina turned toward him again. ''While you were saying goodbye to Reverend Dempsey, my dad gave me...gave *us* a wedding present.''

Clay had a feeling he knew what was coming. ''What was the present?''

There was a pause. ''A check for $5000.''

He told himself not to overreact. Wesley Foster just wanted to make sure his daughter was taken care of. But he had to make himself clear to Gina. ''I won't accept money from your father.''

''It's a wedding present,'' she reminded him.

''No. It's your father's way of keeping his hand in your life.''

She didn't argue the point, and they drove the rest of the way home in silence.

After they arrived at Clay's house, he pulled into the garage and switched off the ignition. They hadn't even had time to move Gina's things over. She'd simply packed a bag for tonight. Tomorrow, her clothes would be hanging next to his in his closet and her presence would become more obvious in his home. He didn't really know how he'd feel about sharing his place with her...living with her. He'd had an apartment in town with Elizabeth because that's where she'd wanted to be. Then she'd pretty much taken it over—cosmetics from one end of the bathroom to the other, decorating everything in the apartment the way she'd wanted it. He'd built his house thinking he'd never marry again, making it comfortable for him. Gina had never even been inside.

As Clay went around the SUV, opened Gina's door for her and took her satchel from the back, he knew she'd glimpsed his house from the lodge. All she'd seen of it was its log exterior with a stone chimney and a peaked roof that had an odd-looking gable. The logs were a deep, dark butternut that blended with the landscape in spring, summer and fall, and stood out against the snow in the winter.

He led her down a short hall past a small laundry room to the kitchen. The room wasn't very big, yet it was functional with its pine cupboards and off-white counters. There was no separation between it and the dining area where an oak table with four chairs stood.

"This is nice," she murmured, looking around.

"It works for me," he said simply.

When he led her into the living room, her eyes swept the more spacious area of pine and cedar and beams. Looking up, she saw the loft bordered by a pole railing. She crossed to the stone fireplace with its hearth and simple beamed mantel as she scanned the teal leather couch and recliner, the braided rug on the plank wood flooring, the colorful wall hanging with its bead work.

"This is so…warm and inviting."

The wrought iron lamps had parchment shades, and he flicked on one of the lights on a pine end table.

He wondered about the house in San Francisco where she'd lived with her father. It was probably much larger.

He pointed down another short hallway. "The powder room is down there. Do you want to see upstairs?"

Her gaze went to the loft. "Sure."

He let her precede him up the stairs. The hall along the railing led into a spacious bedroom with a beamed slanted ceiling. There was a massive lodgepole-pine bed, a pine dresser with mirror and chest and a bear rug on the floor at the foot of the bed. A large picture window faced west. The blind was pulled all the way to the top. There was no one in that direction for miles.

He remarked, "I can watch the sun set from there."

Setting her suitcase on the bed, he pointed to the bathroom. "The bath leads into another bedroom. It's smaller than this one. There's plenty of room in the closet for your things, and the top three drawers of the chest are empty. Two of the dresser drawers are, too."

"That'll be plenty of room," she murmured, glancing around again at the quilted spread that was patterned with trees and snowy mountains.

Gina looked a little lost in the room and now she gave him a tentative smile.

"Would you like to change into something more comfortable?" he asked her. "I know I can't wait to get out of this tux. I could use something to eat, too. Greg and Mary Lou had enough food delivered for a week."

"That sounds good."

He thought Gina looked nervous enough to bolt,

and he didn't know how to make her more at ease. Maybe giving her a little time alone would do that.

"I'll go fix a tray and pop the champagne while you change. Okay?"

She just nodded, and he left her in his bedroom, hoping her tension would diminish as the night went on, hoping they'd be sharing his bed tonight.

As he went to the kitchen and opened the refrigerator, Clay tugged down his bolo tie and unfastened his top shirt button. There was one tray particularly for tonight with sandwiches, fresh vegetables and dip, chocolates and four large chocolate chip cookies. He grabbed that tray, set two plates on top, and took it upstairs. He could hear the shower running in the bathroom. After he set the tray on the nightstand, he returned to the kitchen for the champagne and glasses.

When he entered the bedroom again, Gina was still in the bathroom, and he wondered if she'd ever come out. He decided to make use of the time and undress.

Just as he was reaching for his robe, Gina exited the bathroom and stopped short. She was staring at him, and his body was responding to her. She was beautiful in a white satin gown with tiny little straps that held it on her shoulders. The shimmery material came to her knees, and there was a slit on either side. Her legs and feet were bare and all he wanted to do was go to her and haul her into his arms. He knew better. Restraint and control had never been a problem for him...and they wouldn't be tonight. Whatever happened, he'd deal with it, whether she slept in his bed or not. Reaching for his robe, he slipped it on.

She looked away as if she were embarrassed seeing him naked. He hoped she'd get over that.

He had to pass her on the way to the bathroom. He

stopped beside her, longing to scoop her up into his arms, carry her to the bed and lay her beneath him.

Instead, he said, "I'll be out in a few minutes," and went to get a cold shower.

Five minutes later, Clay emerged from the bathroom, the cold shower not having done much good. Gina was standing by the tray on the nightstand, removing the cover from it. He went to the other nightstand, took the bottle of champagne, and popped the cork. It poured like liquid gold into the glasses.

When he looked across the bed, he caught her gaze. "Do you mind if I take off my robe?"

"No." Her answer was almost a whisper. She was like a deer caught in headlights and he knew he had to put her at ease. Going around to her side of the bed, he sat and patted the mattress next to him.

"Come here," he demanded gently. "I'm afraid you're going to fly away."

She blushed furiously, then lighted beside him. "I'm sorry, Clay. All of this is new to me. I've never done this before and—"

"Did it ever occur to you that I might be glad you haven't done this before?"

Her eyes were so wide and so blue. They reminded him of a clear winter sky as she asked, "You are?"

"It's an honor to be the first man who's intimate with you."

She looked at her hands. "I'm so afraid I'm not going to know what to do."

Taking her chin in his hand, he tipped her head up. "Gina, I won't push you or rush you. If you want to sleep in the spare room tonight, that's fine."

After gazing deeply into his eyes, she said in a low voice, "I don't want to sleep in the spare room."

Her answer fueled his desire and his heart pounded against his ribs. "Then why don't we just start with something easy—like kissing—and see where it takes us."

When he brushed his fingers along her cheek, he was struck all over again by the peachy softness of her skin, the delicacy of her features, the beautiful blue of her eyes. Bending to her slowly, he started with gentleness, pressing lightly then more firmly, eventually coaxing her lips apart. With a soft moan, her arms went around his neck, and he felt stronger and more powerful than he'd ever felt in his life. Clay told himself slow was better. Yet slow was getting to be a damn sight more difficult than he'd expected it to be. As his heart raced, he breathed in Gina's scent, fascinated by her softness. Her response to him was so free. Taking her face between his hands, he pulled away from her.

"What's wrong?" she asked, sounding as breathless as he felt.

"Nothing…if you want to keep on going."

"Do you really want me to be your wife in every way, Clay?"

There were questions in her eyes…questions beyond the obvious that he didn't understand. Maybe he would eventually.

"Yes, I want you to be my wife—in every way." His voice was husky as he said it. "It would be torture to live with you and not sleep with you." Then he took her lips again to show her how much he wanted her. For a moment he felt some hesitation from her, but then her tongue met his and he was shrugging off his robe and taking her down onto the bed.

She's a virgin, Clay reminded himself over and over as he stroked her face and kissed her from her eyes, down her nose, to her lips, then her neck.

"Oh, Clay," she sighed, clasping his shoulders.

"What?" he asked, wanting to make this experience one she'd remember all her life.

"I can't explain it. It feels so wonderful... everywhere."

He chuckled. "That's the idea. It's going to feel even better."

"What can I do for you?" she whispered.

"You're doing it, Gina. Believe me, you're doing it."

When he continued to trail kisses over the mounds of her breasts, she arched up. The satin fabric was like a second skin and he tongued her nipple through it, making the material wet.

She writhed beneath him. "Clay, I can feel that inside...so deep inside."

Her vocal reactions to everything he did were inflaming him more. He could hardly find his voice but finally managed, "Let's take off this nightgown."

When she sat up and he slid it over her head, she looked tousled and so irresistibly shy. Because he was so much bigger than she was, he suggested, "Let's do this another way." Stretching out, he reached for her and pulled her on top of him. She lay full length, gazing into his eyes. He cupped her bottom, stroked the back of her thighs, and kissed her deeply until she was rubbing against him, searching for her first fulfillment as a woman.

He broke the kiss and whispered into her neck, "You know this will hurt at first, don't you?"

He felt her nod, the silkiness of her hair against his

skin, the heat of her body pressed against his. Kissing her again, he reached between them and found her more than ready.

Still he wanted to make sure. He wanted her to be begging for their union so there was no doubt she wanted it as much as he did. That thought startled him. Why did he care so much about that?

His body screamed for release and the thought faded away as he kept kissing her and touching her until she murmured, "Clay, Clay, please. Let's do it."

Again, he had to smile at her innocence, and he realized she had no idea what was coming. He just hoped he could make an orgasm happen for her the first time. He wouldn't let go of his control until he did.

When their bodies glistened from their passion, when the heat between them seemed to fill the room, when he gazed into her very blue eyes and saw she was as involved in their desire as he was, he took a condom from the bedside stand. Straddling his legs, she watched as he slipped it on. Her tongue slid along her lower lip, and he knew he'd never wanted a woman so much. Reaching for her, he took hold of her waist and set her astride him. Then he quickly lowered her onto him, thrusting past the barrier.

She gave a soft cry, but he didn't give her time to think about the breaking of her innocence. Holding her hips, he moved in and out of her, with each thrust a little deeper, until she was contracting around him. Suddenly his control seemed to split in two and he couldn't keep a grasp on it. He'd never lost it before! Never. But as he drove into her faster and faster, as she matched his rhythm, the world as he'd known it seemed to change.

She cried out first and he couldn't control the need of his body to have more of her, to be completely engulfed by her. When his shuddering climax came, it was like nothing he'd ever experienced. His groan seemed to go on and on. All he could see and feel and touch was Gina. His staggering release shook him, and he felt himself drawing her down to him, kissing her until the whirl of colors and sensations, until the explosion of erotic pleasure threatened to tear him apart.

When he could think again...when he could breathe again...he realized he was holding her so tightly he might be hurting her. Opening his eyes, he gazed into hers. What he saw made him freeze. There were tears on her cheeks.

"Did I hurt you?" he asked hoarsely, still shocked his passion had gotten ahead of him, deeply unsettled by an experience he'd never expected.

"No, you didn't hurt me. I never guessed it would be so wonderful. That's all."

Gina's words should have reassured him, but instead he felt more deeply troubled. "It certainly was great sex," he said, almost to himself.

But she heard him and she looked startled. Then she was scurrying off of him and reaching for her nightgown.

This is a marriage of convenience, he told himself. He never should have let himself go like that. It wasn't going to happen again. Gina Foster had married him to make herself independent. Even if she lasted the year, she probably wouldn't stay. She wanted to open a tea room and certainly not in a place like Fairbanks. There was a forecast for snow tomorrow and it only reminded him that soon enough winter would be coming on in earnest.

He needed some distance to figure out what had happened in his bed...in his head...in his body. He'd never reacted to a woman the way he had to Gina tonight, and it unnerved him. He knew better than to start an avalanche that could cause him the same pain he'd experienced when Elizabeth had left.

He saw Gina was turned toward the dresser, belting her robe. Rising to his feet, he said, "I think I'm going to sleep in the guest room tonight."

When she spun around, she looked confused. "Why?"

"Because we need to get used to this marriage a little at a time. Both of us are used to our privacy." He reached for his robe and started for the bathroom.

"You're...you're leaving now? Aren't you hungry?"

As he looked at her, he felt every muscle in his body tense and he was surprised at how exactly hungry he was for her again. He glanced at the food tray. "No. You go ahead, though. I have an early flight tomorrow before the weather moves in, so I'll be up and gone early. Don't feel you have to get up. Just make yourself at home here and when I get back tomorrow I'll help you move your things over. All right?"

She looked so vulnerable standing there, and he wished he could take her into his arms again. But he had to sort a few things out and that wasn't the way to do it.

Finally, she said, "All right. I'll see you tomorrow."

When Clay reached the spare room, he tossed his

robe onto the bed and went to stand at the window. With the glimmer of the moon, he could make out the outline of trees, the crest of the hill. He decided marrying Gina Foster might have been the biggest mistake of his life.

Tears rolled down Gina's face as she sat on the edge of the big bed wondering exactly what had happened. Yet she didn't have to wonder long because she knew. She'd given everything she was to Clay tonight as a reiteration of her marriage vows. The thoughts and feelings and sensations had all taken her by surprise. She'd never expected making love to be so overwhelming.

Obviously Clay's feelings didn't have any part in this. He'd said they'd had great sex, but maybe he was just trying to be nice to her. She hadn't even touched him very much. She hadn't kissed him other than the deep, heart-throbbing kisses he initiated. He'd kissed her everywhere, touched her everywhere. She didn't know anything about men and their reactions.

Taking a deep breath, she got up from the bed and went over to stand at the dresser, looking at her face in the mirror. What could she give this man who was so much more experienced than she was?

With a sigh, she dropped her gaze and saw a sheaf of paper lodged behind the jewelry box. She'd seen papers like that before in her father's home office. It was a sell order for stocks. Then she saw the yellow Post-It note, "$50,000 in escrow for Gina."

This marriage was a business deal for Clay. He was willing to pay to get what he wanted—his inheritance. He had bought her. That was very clear to her now.

Was Clay so very different from Trent? If Trent had married her, he'd have a promotion. Clay married her to get his inheritance. Of course, she had known that going into this marriage, but somehow she'd thought Clay was different, that he cared at least a little. There was no denying the desire in his eyes, but after tonight she realized that's all it had been—desire. She was going to get $50,000. In return, he would secure his inheritance and take advantage of the benefits of marriage...sex.

She dropped her head into her hands. Had she made the worst decision of her life?

Chapter Six

When Mary Lou set the bowl of potato chips on one corner of the card table, she looked from Gina to Clay. "So how's married life?"

Clay glanced at his bride of nine days, not knowing what she'd say. "It's fine."

Gina smiled and he could tell it was a forced smile as she answered simultaneously, "It's fine."

Their first week of married life had been anything but fine. They'd hardly seen each other. But he'd decided it was better that way.

He still couldn't forget making love with Gina, how she'd responded to him, how he'd responded to her. He'd never before lost control like that. He'd never before felt as if everything he was had flowed from him into the woman in his bed.

What had Jed said? *Marriage is never simple.*

Because Clay was determined to get back to simple, he'd slept in the spare room all week. Gina had accepted that, the same way she'd accepted his trip that had kept him away for three days and the long hours he'd spent at the hangar the rest of the time. When Mary Lou had called and asked them to come over and play cards this evening, he'd asked Gina and she'd seemed happy to accept the invitation. Talking with guests at the lodge wasn't the same thing as socializing with friends, and he had the feeling she thought of Mary Lou as a friend. He remembered how he'd come home to Elizabeth who'd gone shopping most days, or gotten her hair done or her nails. She'd hated when he'd flown out of town overnight and she'd complained, "When you're not here, Clay, I don't have anyone to talk to."

Gina wasn't complaining, but then he was going to pay her $50,000 to stay married to him for a year.

Mary Lou exchanged a look with Greg. Her husband glanced from Gina to Clay. "How about more soda?"

Mary Lou frowned, but Greg didn't seem to notice.

After Clay and Gina both declined refills, Greg addressed Gina. "You might see some real Alaskan winter weather this week. The snow we've had up to now hasn't been anything compared to what we're going to get." To Clay he added, "*You* might be grounded for a few days."

"There's always plenty to do at the hangar."

"We're supposed to have guests coming in Tuesday afternoon," Gina murmured, as if thinking out loud.

"The snow's supposed to move in by then. You might have cancellations instead," Greg warned.

"Speaking of getting into winter," Mary Lou interjected with a smile. "Thanksgiving's not too far off. Do you have plans? We'd love it if you'd join us.''

Since he and Gina were treating each other like polite strangers, Clay didn't know what was going to happen by Thanksgiving. ''We'll talk about it and get back to you,'' he told Mary Lou, knowing this was a discussion they'd probably better have in private.

When he looked over at Gina, she picked up her glass and avoided his gaze. This was what happened when a man married for convenience sake. Marriage wasn't convenient at all.

Behind the wheel of her car, Gina drove to Fairbanks on Monday afternoon, unmindful of the gray sky. Although she'd cried herself to sleep a few nights, she told herself she was mature enough to handle whatever this marriage brought her. After all, it had been a risk going into it. Her heart ached because she was in love with Clay and he wasn't in love with her. She wasn't sure he even liked her. When Clay had made love to her on their wedding night, she'd thought he'd been as overwhelmed by the experience as she had. She'd hoped he'd been so gentle and passionate because he was beginning to have feelings for her.

Then he'd turned remote and walked away. Apparently she'd disappointed him because he didn't even seem interested in sex now. Were they going to live the whole year like this? Like uninvolved roommates?

Not even roommates.

Gina thought about Mary Lou's invitation for Thanksgiving. She'd assumed she and Clay would talk about it on the way home. But Clay had just turned on the radio, and she suspected he didn't want to commit himself to the holiday yet. She had the feeling he wished he hadn't married her, and she didn't know what she was going to do about it.

There hadn't been many days Gina had been bored at the lodge, but today she'd been restless. She knew it was because her mind was on Clay, rather than housekeeping or menus or the guests arriving tomorrow. Preparations were finished. Not knowing when Clay would be home, she'd decided to drive into town and deposit the check her father had given her and Clay as a wedding present. She remembered the pride in her husband's voice as he'd told her he wouldn't accept money from her father.

In turmoil, she barely noticed the first snowflakes start to fall as she drove into Fairbanks. When they swirled in front of her instead of landing lightly on her windshield, she remembered what Greg had said about snow coming. Still, she was here now and like a woman on a mission, didn't want to go back to an empty lodge and house. Besides going to the bank, she wanted to buy a new sweater, something Clay would notice so he couldn't walk by her as if she wasn't there.

Gina parked at the mall where the bank she patronized was located. She went there first, then shopped in three different stores looking for just the right sweater. She finally found it. It was turquoise and fuchsia with swirls of color. The sleeves were gathered at the shoulders and it was long, hanging midthigh. She found a pair of turquoise leggings, deciding Clay wouldn't be able to ignore her if she looked so bright. The outfit would be great to wear on Thanksgiving if they went to Mary Lou and

Greg's. She hoped they would. She loved being with them and their children, and she knew Clay did, too. He'd roughhoused with the boys a good part of the evening until the children had gone to bed. He seemed a little more awestruck by Noelle who he'd carefully held and given a ride on his shoulders. She'd giggled and he'd laughed, and Gina had known he'd make a wonderful father.

It was almost five when Gina exited the mall and already dark. The daylight hours were getting shorter. By December twenty-first, night would be about twenty hours long. Stepping outside, she blinked in amazement. The world was covered in white. Not only covered—at least four inches had already fallen. She thought about the small car she'd bought shortly after she'd arrived in Fairbanks. The salesman had sold it to her at a great price but she hadn't driven it in snow yet. She was about to find out how it would handle.

Because she had nothing in the car to wipe away the snow from the windshield, Gina ran the wipers and defroster and used her gloved hands. It took a good fifteen minutes to brush the snow from the hood and the back windshield with her arm. By the time she was finished, at least another inch had covered everything. Snow had fallen over the past few weeks, but not this heavily, not this fast. She knew she had to get on the road and get back. There were some tracks in the parking lot, but not many, and she found herself skidding as she turned out of the lot onto the road.

The main road out of Fairbanks was manageable. If she stayed in the ruts of the other cars, she found she could maneuver just fine. Her car wanted to skid easily, though, and she had to be careful. Her hands were tight on the wheel, her gaze intent on the dark road, not illuminated very brightly by her headlights and the swirling snow. She wondered if Clay had gotten back home yet and if not, where he was. She should have left the mall sooner. But she'd given up hope that he'd be home for dinner and had wanted to fill her time.

When she turned off the main road, she knew she was going to have a problem. The snow was too deep for her car. She managed to drive at least half the distance to the lodge, but then her wheels churned without moving her forward and got stuck. She rocked the car until she could go forward again, but even that stopped working after the next stretch of snow-covered road. After she churned in the deepening white powder for another few yards, she simply couldn't stay straight. She slid to the side of the road and became thoroughly imbedded in the snow on the shoulder. No simple rocking motion would propel her out.

From the distinctive shape of the last house she'd passed with its floodlight on its gabled roof, she guessed she was about a mile from the lodge. That house had been about a mile back. It was silly to walk there when she could walk straight ahead and be home in the same amount of time. After her hiking in Deep River last week, she knew she was in shape. She could do it easily. She was wearing her parka and though she didn't have her hat with the earmuffs, she could put up her hood. Her gloves would keep her hands warm. She was wearing the boots she'd bought for the trip, thank goodness. Even with the snow, she should be able to make Clay's house in half an hour. There was no point sitting here thinking about it.

Gina stuck her purse inside her coat, locked her car doors, and started her trek to Clay's house.

When Clay arrived home around four, he hadn't expected to find Gina gone. It was snowing, and he knew the car she'd bought without asking for anyone's advice wouldn't handle well in anything more than two inches. Already there was more than two inches on the ground.

By five o'clock he was pacing, flicking the TV on and off, paging through a pilot's magazine that right now held no interest. Where in the hell was she? The least she could have done was left a note.

But his conscience reminded him, *You haven't been home before eight any night. Why should she leave a note?*

Frustrated, he went upstairs to the bedroom to take a look around to see if he could figure out where she'd gone. He'd already called Mary Lou and she hadn't heard from her. Murray didn't know where she'd gone today and Joanie wasn't coming in until tomorrow. Who else did she know?

Clay had asked Gina questions about her background, but he should have been finding out more about what she'd done during the past six months. Where did she go when she had days off?

He swore as nothing in the room gave a clue as to her whereabouts. Going into the spare room, he crossed to the window and looked out. The snow wasn't letting up, and by all reports, they'd have at least fifteen inches by morning. The temperature was

only twenty-five. With the wind, it felt more like fifteen.

Where was she? He'd give her another half hour,
then he was calling the State Troopers.

Needing a momentary distraction, he picked up his
grandfather's diary from his bedside table and found
the entry where he'd left off.

> Cora agreed to marry me today. It's the hap-
> piest day of my life. When I told her I'd like to
> move to Deep River and open a trading post
> there, she was all for it. She said even villages
> the size of Deep River need a teacher. She could
> always find somebody to teach. That's one of the
> reasons I love her, one of the things I saw in her
> the first moment I met her. My Cora has spirit
> and heart and isn't afraid to jump into anything
> new. That'll do her good here. That'll do us both
> good.

It was obvious to Clay that his grandfather and his
new bride were a match made in heaven. They'd
jumped in with both feet and fortunately found the
right person for each of them. But how often did that
kind of thing happen now? It certainly didn't happen
when there was money or a will involved.

Clay restlessly closed the diary. Then he brought
more firewood in. He made sure the oil lamps were
nearby and filled. The electricity could go out and he
wanted to be prepared for that.

Taking a deep breath, he thought about Gina again
and was truly worried. Why hadn't she used her cell
phone and called him? Why hadn't she come home?
Her suitcase was still upstairs in the closet, so he

knew she hadn't left for good...unless she'd sponta-
neously decided she'd had enough of him and their
marriage and taken off for San Francisco.

He was about to pick up the receiver to call the
troopers when he thought he heard something outside.
Was it wishful thinking?

No, there was noise on the porch.

Hurrying to the door, he opened it quickly. He
wasn't sure it was Gina at first. The snow-covered
figure wore a parka, the hood covering her head. She
was clutching the neck of her coat as if the parka
hood wouldn't stay up. She looked as if she'd been
rolled in snow and tossed onto his porch. Her lashes
had been down as if she'd been saying a prayer, but
now as they flew up, he saw her clear blue eyes.

He rushed toward her. "Gina. What happened?"

When he took her by the elbow, she seemed to
have trouble walking across the porch. Swearing, he
swept her up into his arms and carried her inside,
pushing the door shut with his foot. It banged but he
hardly noticed as he carried her into the living room
in front of the fireplace. The snow was already melt-
ing, dripping onto the braided rug, but he didn't care.
He had to know how long she'd been out there.

"What happened?" he asked again.

When she tried to talk, her teeth chattered. "I...
g-g-got stuck in the snow."

"You didn't have your cell phone?"

"It's...it's at the lodge," she mumbled.

"Great place for it, Gina. How far did you walk?"

"About a mile...I...think." Her words were
bumpy.

He brushed back her parka hood and looked at her
face, rubbing his thumbs over her cheeks. They were

ice cold, but they were pink, not white, so he didn't think she'd gotten any frostbite. Her large hood had protected her. Next he took off her gloves. She just stood there like a statue...frozen...and he suspected she probably was. He took one of her hands in his and rubbed it between his large ones, hoping to get her circulation flowing faster.

"Oh, that feels good."

The look on her face, the huskiness in her voice made him want to take her into his arms and kiss her. But he had to get her warm and make sure she was really all right. Drawing off the other glove, he did the same thing with her other hand.

Quickly he unzipped her parka and shoved it from her shoulders. Then he ordered, "Take off your jeans. They're caked with snow."

For a moment her gaze met his, her eyes wide.

"Gina, I've seen you undressed. This is no time for modesty. I want to make sure you haven't gotten any frostbite. It's only twenty-five degrees out there."

"I'm sorry. I never meant to be such a bother."

Again he swore, not even sure why he was so frustrated. Because of her stupidity? Possibly. But his gut told him there was more, too. A lot more.

She tried to unfasten her jeans, but her fingers didn't seem to want to work. He took over for her, unsnapping and unzipping them, finally pushing them down her hips. She avoided his gaze, and he told himself this was no time to admire her curvy legs.

"Sit," he ordered pushing her gently onto the sofa.

Then he yanked off her boots, one by one, and unpeeled her stockings. At least she'd worn a double wool layer there. When the jeans huddled in a pile on top of her parka, he took the afghan from the back of the sofa and wrapped it around her. Kneeling in front of her, taking her feet into his hands, he rubbed warmth into them.

"Where were you?"

"At the mall."

He gave a grunt of disgust. *Just like Elizabeth.* "And you had such important shopping to do you ignored the snow?"

"I was halfway there when it started snowing lightly. I never expected it to mount up like this so quickly."

Shaking his head, he swung her legs up onto the sofa. "I'll be right back with something hot."

It was the fastest hot chocolate he ever made, and he returned to the living room in less than five minutes. "Drink it," he said pushing it toward her. "It's not steaming so you don't have to worry about burning yourself."

Sitting at her feet, he knew he had to make an impression on her, to let her know exactly what could have happened tonight. "Gina, I'm going to say this once and I want you to remember it. You could have died out there."

Her cheeks, which had started becoming pinker, suddenly went pale again. "I knew it was only a mile. I...I knew I was in shape."

"No one's in shape for a blizzard. *Never* leave your vehicle. Do you understand me? *Never.* What if you'd lost your way and ended up a mile in the other direction?"

"I followed road markers and telephone poles and the tree line."

"Well, I'm glad something worked because your common sense sure didn't. You should have turned back when you saw it starting to snow. At the least, when you came out of the mall and saw what it was like, you should have stayed in Fairbanks and for God's sake, realized that car of yours would be of no earthly use here in the winter.''

"Clay, I'm sorry. I…'' Her teeth were still chattering and now tears rolled down her cheeks.

He felt like a complete cad. He hadn't wanted to make her cry, but she had to understand the seriousness of what she'd done. The mug of chocolate trembled in her hand, and he didn't know if she was shaking from what he'd said or if she was still that cold. There was only one way to really get her warm.

Taking the chocolate from her, he set it on the table, then he scooped her up into his arms and headed for the stairs.

"What are you doing?''

"I've got to get you warm. Body heat will do that best.''

"B…b…body heat?''

"Yes. Yours and mine. Under the covers.''

Once in his bedroom, he stood her by the side of the bed, then yanked back the covers and stripped off the afghan covering her. "Take off your clothes and get in.''

"But Clay…''

"Don't argue with me, Gina. Rely on my good sense tonight, okay?''

As if she'd realized she'd been incredibly foolish, she didn't argue but quickly stripped off her sweater and bra as she shivered. Finally, she slipped off her panties.

Turning around, Clay glanced over his shoulder while he stripped off his own clothes. She scurried into bed before he'd finished. He lifted the flannel sheet, blanket and spread, then slid beneath them.

The bed was huge, and she was over on the other side. He could sense her shivering and knew it would probably take all night until she got warm again.

His frustration and anger gone now, he gently crooked his finger at her. "Come here. I'm just going to hold you and get you warm. You'll be shivering all night otherwise."

She looked at him with trusting blue eyes that told him she'd do whatever he said. As she slid toward him, he extended his arm and snuggled her close to him. "Relax," he said, breathing in her hair and the cold and Gina.

She was still shivering. "I...I can't."

"Think of someplace warm, a Malibu beach maybe, the sun beating down on you." His heart pounded hard in the silence and he wondered if she could hear it. "I'm sorry I yelled at you. I just couldn't believe you'd done something so foolish."

There was a long pause until she murmured, "It's okay. I thought I was doing the best thing. I didn't know—" She shook her head.

His chin was nestled in her hair and he rubbed it back and forth. "I'm going to have to give you a primer on winter in Alaska and how to handle it. I didn't expect you to be out when it started snowing."

"I've never been in a blizzard before," she confessed in a small voice against his shoulder.

Sometimes he forgot exactly how sheltered she'd been. He stroked her hair. "It's okay. You're safe now. I'll make sure that never happens again. The first thing we're going to do is get you a car you can depend on."

"It was what I could afford."

"We're married, Gina. I'll take care of whatever you need."

She pulled away from him then and looked up at him. "This past week you didn't act as if we were married."

A few moments of heavy silence ticked by along with his heartbeats. "I've been trying to sort some things out. I thought maybe you were, too."

She kept her gaze steady on his. "What were you trying to sort out?"

"What kind of marriage we're going to have. If you're going to leave after the year, distance between us might be a good thing."

Her eyes were huge, her lower lip a bit tremulous as she asked, "And what if I don't leave after a year?"

"You'd open a tea room in Fairbanks? I'm not sure that would go over as well here as in San Francisco or Seattle."

"Alaskans don't drink tea?" she asked with one of the smiles he liked so much.

"You know what I mean," he said seriously. It was more than the tea room and she knew it, too.

"You're afraid I'm not suited for Alaska. You're afraid tonight's going to scare me just like the bear did."

"Isn't it?"

"I don't know, Clay. I need time to adjust to all of this, just as anyone would in a place they weren't used to."

There was truth in that. But he didn't think adjustment to Alaska was that easy.

She shivered again in his arms and he nudged her

back onto his shoulder. "Before we try to solve any of this, let's get you warm."

When Gina awakened, there weren't any lights on in the room. She was snuggled into Clay's powerful body. Her head rested on his broad shoulder, her arm hugged his chest, her hand was tucked beneath his back. She was pressed against him for warmth, and her legs were practically wrapped around his thigh. She'd never been so cold in her life. She'd never been so scared in her life. After she'd started out on her walk, she couldn't see behind her and she could hardly see in front of her. If it hadn't been for the tree line and telephone poles, Clay had been right— she wouldn't have known which direction to walk. Her attempt at being brave and independent could have been the most foolish thing she'd ever done.

But she was warm now. Her cheek registered the texture of Clay's skin, and she couldn't help but rub it back and forth just a little, remembering the night they'd made love.

"Are you awake?" Clay's husky voice startled her.

She was tempted to lay perfectly still, to pretend she was still asleep so he wouldn't move away from her. But she couldn't pretend with Clay. "Yes."

"Are you warm now?" His deep voice had a strained quality.

"Yes. Thank you for…for doing this."

"I didn't do anything," he muttered. "But I might if I don't go to the spare room."

Did that mean he wanted her? Or was any woman's body this close to him simply a temptation? Taking all of her courage into her hands, she said in a small voice, "You don't have to."

There was silence and finally, ''This is going to get real complicated if I stay.''

''You mean our marriage?''

''Yes.''

Then she did something she never thought she'd do. She couldn't see him very well in the darkness, but she sensed the shadow of his profile. ''I want you to stay, Clay. Why shouldn't we make this marriage a real one? Unless you don't want me. I know I don't have very much experience—''

He swore viciously. ''Your lack of experience is what turns me on.''

Then his hand slid under her hair as he tipped up her face and devoured her mouth with his. She wasn't sure what he meant, what she was doing right, but the moment his tongue delved into her mouth, she couldn't think.

The sheer blackness in the room along with the blizzard outside seemed to enhance what was happening between them. Her hands moved over Clay, exploring him as she'd wanted to ever since their wedding night. She'd been almost afraid to touch him that night, afraid she'd do something wrong. But tonight, for this moment, he was hers and he seemed to like whatever she did.

His low groan when her fingers grazed his nipple urged her to do it again, to stroke her tongue against his, to press her body even closer so their skin seemed not to belong to one or the other but to both of them. Gina discovered hard muscles that were always hidden beneath Clay's clothes. Just by her touch, she realized how fit he was, how virile, how he could dominate without even trying. Yet he wasn't that kind

of man and she realized that's why she trusted him
so.

Clay's hands were large and male as they passed
down her back and caressed her bottom. Shivers
broke out up and down her spine, and they had nothing to do with being cold. She was hot to her very
core. But tonight was about more than heat. She
wanted Clay to commit to making this marriage a real
one. He might not love her, yet tonight proved that
he cared about her. She'd seen the worry on his face
and could feel his anger at her foolishness as much
as his body heat as he lay beside her.

Yes, he cared about her.

The silence in the room was a velvet backdrop for
their sighs and low moans. Clay brought his lips to
her breasts for the first time, and she felt as if she'd
burst from the pleasure of it. She cupped him in her
hands, awed by his male power.

She realized Clay was at the end of his tether when
he rolled her over and rose up on top of her, kissing
her as if he wanted it to go on forever. When he thrust
into her, she arched up to receive him. The sensations
in her body became almost too much for her to grasp.
It was as if a series of tiny explosions began in her
limbs, centered in her womb, and then burst into a
giant cataclysmic climax that seemed to shake the
room. Her cry became muffled by another of Clay's
kisses and then he was shuddering against her and
she knew the explosion had rocked him, too.

She wanted to hold on to him forever. As soon as
he caught his breath, he rolled to her side, then gathered her close to him. She wanted him to tell her what
making love had meant to him. She wanted him to

say he'd been as affected as she was. But he didn't do either. Though he held her, he was silent.

She decided sleeping in his arms would be enough... for tonight.

Chapter Seven

In the early morning, Gina felt Clay stir. He'd moved away from her during the night, but not so far that she couldn't move her leg and feel his...or hear the sound of his breathing.

Now she knew he was going to try to get up without awakening her. "Clay?" she asked, turning toward his side of the bed, finding his face in the shadows.

"I have to see to snow removal." His voice was brusque.

She pushed herself up, fully awake now, and turned on the bedside lamp. "I'll make you breakfast."

Sitting on the bed, he glanced over his shoulder. "You don't have to do that."

"I know I don't have to. I want to." When he was silent, she asked, "What's wrong?"

As he shifted toward her, his troubled brown gaze met hers. "We didn't use protection last night."

She remembered how they'd come together, how

it had been fast and hot and unthinking. "No, we didn't," she said in a low voice.

"I meant what I said before we got married. If you get pregnant and you leave Alaska, the child stays with me."

"You seem so sure I'm going to leave."

"Anything can happen in a year. And life here is—" He stopped. "Look how unprepared you were for this blizzard."

"I learned my lesson. Now I know I can't start out as I did. Now I know I have to take precautions. I've never lived with weather like this before."

He raked his hand through his hair. "Until spring comes, you might be good and tired of it. The point is, Gina, we can't let what happened last night happen again. I won't let it happen again."

"It's not all your responsibility. We're partners in this, aren't we?"

Rising from the bed, he picked up his shirt and jeans that he'd tossed to the floor last night. "I think this has gotten a lot more complicated than either of us expected."

"Do you regret what happened last night?" she asked, forcing the issue.

"I regret we didn't use protection."

"I don't mean that, Clay."

Facing her, he looked troubled. "You were vulnerable last night. I took advantage of that."

So *that's* what was wrong. He was trying to protect her. She didn't want to *be* protected from him. "You might be older than I am, Clay, but you don't have to be my protector. I knew what I wanted last night as much as you did."

There was quiet in the snowy morning until he asked, "And what will you want tonight, Gina?"

She felt naked emotionally as well as physically but knew they needed honesty between them. "I want you to…to sleep with me." Not knowing how else to say it, she'd used the euphemism.

"If I share this bed with you," Clay said gruffly, "we're going to do more than sleep."

She was in love with Clay, and she wanted to give him that love. She knew his feelings didn't go deeper than desire, but she was hoping in time that they would. After all, she had a year. "Our marriage is already more than a simple agreement. I don't think there's any going back."

Silent for a few moments, he finally admitted, "Maybe not. But we can be damn careful going forward. Your dad's not going to stop trying to convince you to go back to San Francisco. If it was up to him, he'd have this marriage annulled and you'd be back under his roof."

"He hasn't convinced me so far. Why can't you trust me?"

Avoiding her gaze, he looked out the window as if seeing the past and the pain it had brought him. "I don't trust anyone but myself. That's the way it has to be out here."

She hadn't realized how deep Clay's mistrust went. His mother had torn him away from his father, had taken him away from a place he loved. His wife had walked out. She'd just have to prove to him that he *could* trust her.

A week later, Gina wasn't sure she'd made any progress in earning Clay's trust. They went to bed together every night, and his lovemaking was fiery, yet patient and giving, too. Still, she could feel him holding himself in check. He wouldn't let go completely. He wouldn't give to her everything he was. Now she realized why.

She had to show him she was part of his life and would stay a part of his life. There wasn't any grand gesture she could make, but there were lots of little ones. She was going to start by warming up his house and making her presence known. The log home was comfortable, but she could tell he didn't spend much time there. She wanted to make it a haven for them...a place where they shared a life.

After the roads had been cleared of snow and traffic started moving again, Clay had driven with her into Fairbanks and they'd traded in her car. To Clay's surprise, she'd chosen a four-wheel drive pickup truck that was six years old, but in good condition. He'd checked it out himself and told her with a few adjustments, it should be reliable. She'd used most of her savings she'd brought to Alaska for it, though Clay had wanted to buy it for her. She decided it was better if she paid for it herself. She'd taken the pickup out a few times with Clay and now she was comfortable with it as she drove to Fairbanks. She intended to use some of the wedding present from her father to decorate his house. No matter what Clay said, that money belonged to both of them. His walls were mostly bare, and there were no knickknacks sitting around. It was strictly a bachelor pad. She wanted to change that.

Remembering an art gallery she'd seen in the strip mall, she headed that way. By afternoon, she'd bought two framed canvases for the walls, a colorful lamp, floor rugs, a food processor and a good cutlery set. Clay had told her he'd be back around six today. She wanted to have everything in the house arranged and supper ready, too. Although it wasn't good for business, she was glad their guests had canceled this week.

By six o'clock she'd placed the rugs on the floor in the foyer and in front of the TV. One painting hung above the sofa, the other on the wall leading up the stairway. She'd made a hearty chicken stew, a chocolate cream pie and biscuits. When the front door opened, she was surprised Clay hadn't used the garage entrance. But she was ready for him.

She heard his boots in the foyer and then he stopped, took a few steps into the living room, and then stopped again. Taking a bolstering breath, she went in to greet him.

He was standing in the center of the room, looking around at the changes she'd made. She'd shifted a chair, moved a table, added the knickknacks. She noticed he'd brought the mail in and was carrying a package.

"What do you think?" she asked eagerly.

"You've made some changes."

She couldn't tell from his tone if he was pleased or not. "I thought I'd brighten the house up a bit." She pointed to the lamp. "More light when the nights get longer." She gestured to the paintings. "They bring out the colors in the afghan and the chair over there."

"I see. Did you put all this on the credit card I gave you?"

Clay had given her one of his credit cards to use for groceries and any other necessities.

This is where it got a little sticky. "No, I didn't."

"You used your money? I thought the truck took all that."

"Practically, but… I deposited the check Dad gave me for our wedding present. I used that."

Clay's eyes grew stormy as he looked around the room again. "You shouldn't have. I told you I don't want your father's money."

How could she explain so he'd understand? "I wanted to do something…for us."

"*Not* with your father's money," he said angrily. "It's a matter of principle, Gina."

He set the mail on the coffee table. "There's a package there for you from Ben. I'm going to go over to the lodge and make sure everything's secure and then back to the hangar."

She could tell him she'd made dinner for him, but she wasn't going to beg him to stay. She had *her* pride, too, and it was about time she used it to protect herself. Still, she couldn't help but ask, "When will you be back?"

"I don't know. I'll call if I'm going to be there overnight."

"At the hangar?"

"I bunk with Dave when I get waylaid there. If I don't call, I'll be back."

It was true she didn't know much about men, but she knew something about Clay. He didn't want to feel anything for her. He was barricading himself against anything they could have together, and she didn't know how to get through that barricade. Instead of telling him she wanted to share dinner with him, instead of telling him she wanted to go to bed with him, she simply said, "I'll see you later then...or tomorrow morning."

Clay turned around and left again without even unzipping his parka.

The sky was clear, the stars crystal bright, the moon high and round as Clay parked in the garage and came inside. He'd parked out front when he'd come home at six knowing he was going to leave again. He'd expected to have dinner with Gina first, but she'd surprised him with everything she'd bought for the house. He was still unsettled by the desire he felt for her that only got stronger instead of lessening. He didn't know why, anymore than he knew why he felt he had to keep his defenses invincible, his guard up. He couldn't remember a woman ever getting to him like this.

As he started into the kitchen, he could smell lingering aromas—cooked meat, something baked. There was a piece of paper taped to the cupboard next to the sink. He went over to it.

Clay—If you haven't eaten, there's stew in the refrigerator along with chocolate cream pie. Biscuits are in the bread box. Gina

He almost groaned, feeling like a heel. She'd gone to a lot of trouble and he'd left without even tasting any of it. No, he hadn't eaten supper, but he wasn't hungry now, either. He had fences to mend with her.

He left his parka and scarf on the kitchen chair, turned off the kitchen light and went into the living room. The new lamp was glowing. He saw it as a bit of defiance on her part, and he almost smiled. Taking the stairs quickly, he hoped she was still up. When he saw the closed door, he knew she wasn't. He also knew that closed door was a symbol of what had happened between them. He'd upset her. He'd seen it in her blue eyes. But she'd toughed it out, and he realized she had pride the same as he did.

When he opened the door and went into the bedroom, he saw Gina was turned on her side...away from him. He didn't want to wake her if she was asleep. Already his body was responding to the thought of climbing into bed with her. He'd almost given up trying to fight the attraction, yet he couldn't give into it completely, either. There was too much at stake. When Elizabeth had left, he'd felt betrayed...deceived...stupid. He never wanted to feel any of that again.

Discarding his clothes noiselessly, he draped them over the bedside chair then slid into bed. Gina still didn't move and he knew in his gut that she wouldn't. It was up to him to right this.

He shifted closer to her then lay on his side behind her, wrapping his arm around her. "Gina?" he whispered.

She turned in his arms.

"I saw the supper you made. I'm sorry I didn't stay for it."

As he gazed down at her, the moon shining through the window cast light on her pretty face. Suddenly he realized he'd reacted as he had because he saw her father's money and her old lifestyle as a threat that could take her away from him, away from the marriage before the year was up...as well as *after* the year was up.

"Do you want me to take back everything I bought?" she asked softly.

With a sigh, he shook his head. "No. If it makes you happy, you should keep it."

"Making this house a home for us is what makes me happy."

He heard the sincerity in her voice. "I shouldn't have ruined your surprise," he said roughly.

"It's okay." Her words sounded shaky, and he suspected she was still upset.

"No, it's not okay. Let me make it up to you." Then he bent his head to kiss her, determined to enjoy whatever they had...for as long as they had it.

When Clay pulled into the parking lot at the Gold Rush Saloon on the outskirts of Fairbanks on the Friday after Thanksgiving, Gina felt almost lighthearted. During the past two weeks, she and Clay had settled into their life together. His house now felt like home, and the nights she spent in his bed gave her hope for a future with him, even though he was still holding back, even though he was still guarded. They'd spent Thanksgiving Day with Mary Lou, Greg and the kids and it had been relaxing and fun. Tonight, pilots Clay knew were having a party in the Gold Rush's back room. It was a yearly tradition. She was looking forward to it. She knew Joanie would be here because she was dating Dave Wagner. At least Gina would know someone other than Clay.

After Clay parked the car, he came around to her door and helped her out. "I forgot to tell you but it's an "Oldies" theme tonight. Do you know how to jitterbug?"

Before she had time to answer, he added, "Of

course you do. I'll bet you had dancing classes at that boarding school.''

"I had dancing classes—everything from square dancing to the tango. But I've never had much chance to practice. How about you?''

He closed her door and pressed the remote to lock the car. Then he automatically took her arm to help her across the icy parking lot. "I did my share of dancing. Not the tango, though. I joined a dance club one winter. It was a good place to go to spend Saturday night.''

And to meet women, Gina thought.

Distracted by the thought, she almost slipped in her black dress-boots with their higher heel. Clay took a firmer grip on her arm. "Those boots aren't much use on ice and snow.''

"I know, but I wanted to dress up a little tonight. I get tired of jeans.''

"That's what everybody will probably be wearing.''

She hadn't even thought to ask Clay about that. She'd seen tonight as a date and an opportunity to look nice for him as well as for herself. She'd worn a royal blue cashmere turtleneck and matching wool-blend slacks. Now she wondered if she'd stick out like a sore thumb.

Although Clay eased his protective grip on her arm, she could still feel the branding imprint of his fingers. She knew that was impossible through the down of her coat, but she could feel it nevertheless, just as she could feel the dancing electricity that always tingled between them.

"How do you like these?'' he asked, brushing his

finger over the beaded moosehide gloves Ben had sent her.

"They're beautiful. And warm. The fact that he sewed them himself makes them even more special. They're a generous gift."

"Ben's a generous man. He taught me how to listen to the wind, track a bear, find the best berry bushes. Dad took me to Deep River often when I first moved back here."

They'd reached the building, and Clay pulled open the heavy wooden door. Gina saw a bar to one side and a restaurant to the other. Clay's hand came to rest at the small of her back as he guided her. "This way."

They threaded their way through the restaurant into a large back room with three long tables, folding chairs, and a stereo setup with speakers. An Elvis song was playing and at least twenty people milled about. Joanie waved from the table where she sat with Dave. He motioned to the two vacant chairs there.

As Gina and Clay approached them, the russet-haired maintenance man grinned at them. "We warmed up the seats for you. Just need your order to get the night started."

"Root beer for me," Clay said.

Gina knew Clay didn't drink when he was flying or driving. "That's fine for me, too."

Joanie nodded to the bowls of chips and nuts on the table. "We ordered a few pizzas. They should be out shortly."

"Sounds good," Clay said as he helped Gina remove her coat and hung it on the back of the chair.

For the next half hour, Gina spoke with Clay's friends and their wives or dates, getting to know them.

Everyone was wearing jeans, and at first she did feel out of place. Yet nobody seemed to care and soon she relaxed, listening to Paul Simmons recount a story about an eccentric client.

When an old Paul Anka tune started playing, Joanie looked at Dave. "Want to dance?"

He took her hand and they went to the area of the floor where couples were already dancing.

Clay gazed at Gina. "How about you?"

She nodded. Clay's affection and passion were confined to the bedroom. She wasn't sure why unless he was trying to keep his desire compartmentalized so their marriage didn't invade every aspect of his life. He was at the hangar or flying most of the day while she worked at the lodge. In the evenings he checked weather charts, consulted with clients, or read pilots' magazines while she worked a latch-hook rug she'd found in a craft store. In a way, they were housemates. Yet whenever his gaze caught hers, or whenever they inadvertently touched, she knew they were so much more.

Clay took her into his arms, not leaving much distance between them. When he guided her in a traditional box step, his thighs pressed hers, his lips whispered near her temple, and her cheek brushed the cableknit of his tan sweater. When the Anka song ended, a Frankie Avalon one followed.

"Gina," Clay said, his voice rough.

She looked up at him.

"I think we'd better sit out the slow dances and wait for a jitterbug."

"Why?"

He pressed against her. "That's why. This seems too much like foreplay."

Knowing he was aroused excited her. "Do you want to go home now?" she asked, lifting her lashes, realizing she was flirting with him.

His brown eyes became darker with the thought. "We haven't been here very long. I thought you'd enjoy seeing someone other than me."

"We can leave whenever you want." She wanted him to know that he was enough for her, and she didn't need a country club or a bridge group or anything that he thought went with her old lifestyle.

"We'll give it a little longer," he decided with a crooked grin. "I wouldn't want to miss doing the jitterbug with you."

When the song ended, they went back to the table. Joanie was asking Clay if he was going to make any renovations in the lodge this year when Dave nudged his arm. Clay looked up and his gaze fell on the woman crossing to the table. She came around to Clay and smiled at him.

Gina instantly went on alert. The woman was lithe in jeans and a green Henley shirt. She had straight blond hair cut chin-length and dark brown eyes that held more than friendship for Clay.

"Would you like to dance?" she asked Clay.

Clay stood and his hand went to Gina's shoulder. "Hi, Maggie. Maggie Costain, meet my wife, Gina."

Maggie was more than astonished, maybe even a little shocked. "Wow! I see while I was getting a divorce, you were getting married. Good to meet you, Gina. Would you mind if I dance with your husband?"

Gina had been taught well how to be a lady. Though she felt anything but gracious, she lied, "Of course I don't mind."

Clay's gaze caught hers. She gave him a reassuring smile.

At that, Maggie put her hand on Clay's arm and the two walked to the dance floor.

Gina couldn't help watching them as Clay took Maggie into his arms as if he'd done it before. The way they were looking at each other, Gina suspected they were more than old friends.

"Don't stare," Joanie said in an aside to Gina.

Flustered now, Gina glanced at the waitress. "Have they known each other a long time?"

"About a year and a half."

"Were they involved?" Gina couldn't let her pride get in the way of knowing the truth.

"That depends what you mean by involved. Maggie's a pilot. Clay met her on one of his trips to Juneau. He brought her to this party last year when she came to visit for a few days. Everyone could see they were suited to each other. But that night, Clay found out she wasn't divorced, just separated. I think she and her husband were trying to work things out. So Clay backed off and didn't see her again after that."

Suited to each other. Gina could see that they were. The woman was five-ten, not only beautiful, but fit, too. A pilot.

"Is she from here? Alaska, I mean?" Gina asked.

"Oh, yeah. Her grandfather came here looking for gold. She's lived in Juneau all her life."

And now she was free, Gina thought. What was Clay thinking and feeling? If he had known…

Would he have asked Maggie Costain to marry him? Gina had the feeling it wouldn't have been a marriage for convenience sake only.

All of her insecurities came back to haunt her.

Maybe Clay was simply marking time with her and after the year, he wouldn't want her around anymore. Then he could start a real life with Maggie.

Suddenly it was too warm in the room, and Gina felt nauseous. She needed to see the sky, she needed to be out in the open. She needed to be away from everyone who knew Clay had feelings for Maggie Costain.

Grabbing her parka, she said to Joanie, "I'll be back in a few minutes," and then before the waitress could ask where she was going, she was through the dining room and out the front door.

The cold hit her, and she filled her lungs with it. It was so different than the foggy damp air of San Francisco. Here, everything seemed brighter, bigger, untamed...including all her feelings for Clay.

She went to the side of the porch and held on to the railing. Heaven help her, she loved Clay and the feeling was more intense than any she'd ever experienced.

"What are you doing out here?" Her husband's deep voice carried in the clear night. He was wearing his parka, but it was unzipped as he came over to stand beside her.

"I needed some fresh air."

"I see."

They looked up at the sky together now and Gina wondered if she was seeing things. There were opalescent ripples against the black.

"You picked a good night for stargazing. Those are the Northern Lights."

"They're beautiful," she said, tears coming to her eyes, her love for Clay and the magic of something so otherworldly overwhelming her.

"Some nights they're even more distinct. I'll watch for them so you can see them in all their glory."

"I can watch myself." She wanted him to know he didn't have to take care of her. She wanted to be his equal. She didn't want him always thinking of her as a tenderfoot and inexperienced. And she knew she had to ask him what was on her mind.

"Were you and Maggie lovers?"

At first she thought Clay's silence was going to be her only answer. "You asked me about Trent," she reminded him. "I want to know about Maggie."

He still gazed at the beautiful streaks in the sky. "I met her on a trip to Juneau. I got snowed in there and we spent some time together."

"Time dating?"

"We had a lot in common."

"Because she's a pilot?"

"Yes."

"But it got more serious than that."

The night seemed to pulse with each moment that passed. "I wanted it to get more serious. She flew down here last year and came to this party with me. I took her back to my house. I'd just finished it then. I opened a bottle of wine, we had a few glasses and I found out she was separated, not divorced. She and her husband were in counseling together. I knew better than to tamper with someone else's marriage. She slept in the guest room, and I brought her back to town in the morning. That was the last time we saw each other."

"Until tonight," Gina noted. "If you had known she'd gotten a divorce you could have married *her*."

Finally, Clay turned to her. "I married *you*, Gina."

"If Maggie had been free, would you still have asked me to marry you?"

The colorful pearl fingers waved toward heaven. "I don't know."

Gina had hoped he was coming to love her. She had hoped they were creating bonds that would last. Now she knew he was probably just putting in time. After a year, he could do whatever he wanted. He'd have his inheritance and he'd probably want a divorce.

"I think I'd like to go home."

"Gina…"

"Really, Clay. My stomach's a little queasy. Too much pizza. Can we go now?"

He took her face between his palms. "Do you think you're coming down with something?"

She knew she was—a good old case of jealousy. "I'll be fine. A good night's sleep will do the trick."

If she could snuggle up with Clay beside her and lie in his arms, maybe she wouldn't feel so desolate inside.

Chapter Eight

Taking the last of the furniture out of the guest bedroom on Sunday morning and placing it in the room next door, Clay went to the top of the stairs and called, "Gina?"

She'd been fairly quiet ever since the dance on Friday...ever since she'd asked him about Maggie. He'd told her the truth. If he'd known Maggie had been free before the lawyer told him the terms of his father's will, maybe he *would* have asked her to marry him. Yet he couldn't quite imagine it. Maggie Costain was the original pioneer woman. Yes, they had a lot in common. Maybe too much. Her life was her plane. Clay's was, too, to a certain extent. Yet the idea of him and Maggie married just didn't sit well.

He thought of the last entry from the 1930s he'd read in his grandfather's diary.

I can't get much for furs anymore. The Depression's done that. The Depression's almost put us out of business. I've been giving credit when I shouldn't, but no one else has any more money than I do. Cora's been great about all of it. She says we'll be fine, that we just have to ride it out, that we can live on biscuits and fish if we have to. I want to give her more than that, but she says as long as we're together, nothing else matters. Never thought I'd believe in stuff like that, but I think she's right.

From the diary, Clay could see that his grandfather and grandmother had something special. His grandmother had been an adventurer like his grandfather, loving the untamed quality about Alaska. So did Maggie. Then why couldn't he picture himself married to her? Why could he only picture himself married to Gina?

Gina came running up the steps then. Today she was wearing leggings and a long sweater, the same outfit she'd worn on Thanksgiving. That sweater was an eye-catcher, and he thought it was a little too nice for wallpapering one of the guest rooms. Maybe he thought it was a little too nice because it turned him on as much as everything else she wore.

"Are you sure you want to help with this?" he asked her. If they were bumping into each other, he was going to be distracted.

"I can help. I set aside today for this. Tomorrow I'll inventory the closets and go through the bedding. What do we do first?"

First, he wanted to kiss her and take her back to the house to their bedroom. But he couldn't let himself want her too much. He couldn't let himself need her too much. He'd heard her talking to her father last night. Foster was still trying to get her to come back to San Francisco, and Clay knew he wouldn't give up. He was that kind of man. She might stick out the year to get the $50,000. After that, he knew he couldn't count on her staying.

After they established a plumb line on the wall, Clay filled the wallpaper trough with water. Gina stood by as they booked the paper. Once they got started, they wouldn't have time to gaze at each other or long to fill the silence with something other than the sounds of work.

Still, as they hung one strip of paper after another, distractions abounded. As Clay stood on the step stool with Gina not far beneath him, their arms brushed. He could smell her shampoo and see her silky curls caress her cheek. The close proximity was driving him crazy. Every night since she'd gotten caught in the blizzard, they'd made love. He'd never had that kind of constant physical satisfaction before. Yet he wanted more of her. It didn't make sense.

They'd almost completed one wall when Gina bent over and smoothed the paper near the floor. Then suddenly, she clasped his thigh to steady herself.

He took hold of her shoulders and brought her up to him. "Are you okay?" He thought she looked a little pale.

"I'm fine. Just lost my balance for a second."

She looked so pretty. Clay couldn't turn away from her, and she couldn't seem to look away from him. "Gina," he said, his voice husky, her name barely audible.

Her eyes were luminous and filled with emotion. He didn't want her to be upset about Maggie, and if she was still bothered by his dance with the pilot, he wanted to clear that away.

"Friday night you asked me if I would have married Maggie if she'd been free. I probably would have considered it. Maybe I would have done it if you hadn't been here. The truth is—I'm glad I married you. Maggie's off flying as much as I am and when she's not, she's helping to train huskies. I get the feeling she doesn't like being home. I could never see her sitting and sewing like you do, cooking, decorating her house."

The silence in the room was filled with the beat of his heart.

"You're glad you married me?" Gina asked tentatively.

Truthfully, he admitted, "I didn't like being forced into marriage. But since I was... Yes, I'm glad I married you. Can't you tell?" Then his lips were on hers and they were lost in a kiss he knew wouldn't stop there.

Suddenly Clay remembered the first time he'd taken a plane up. That takeoff was a sensation he'd never forget. Making love to Gina was like that. She was the wind that took his desire to a height he'd never imagined. Her sweet kisses were so freely given. Now as his tongue delved deeply into her mouth, her hands slid under his sweatshirt and up his chest. His body shuddered and he knew her touch was more potent, more exhilarating than flying above the clouds.

After he lifted his sweatshirt over his head and tossed it onto the carpet, he tugged her sweater up and over her head, too. She was wearing a lacy bra. He just marveled at the daintiness of it...the daintiness of her. After he unclasped her bra, he bent his head to her nipple and tongued it.

She arched toward him. "Clay, that feels so wonderful."

She always told him how good he made her feel and that urged him to do even more. "The floor's going to be hard," he murmured when he raised his head.

"It doesn't matter," she said breathlessly.

When they fell to their knees, Clay was still kissing her and Gina was holding on to him. She quivered when he caressed her breast. When she brushed her hands across his stomach, around to his back and slid them into his waistband, he knew he couldn't last much longer. He also knew he needed her too damn much. That need was dangerous.

"Gina," he groaned.

"I love when you say my name like that," she murmured.

He said it again.

Her hands went to his belt, his went to her leggings. They collapsed onto the floor undressing each other, reaching for each other, touching each other.

"I'm glad I have my wallet in my jeans," he said wryly as he reached for it and the condom.

She'd become bolder each time they'd made love and now her hands slid over his aching arousal.

"Gina, wait, or it'll be all over before—"

"It doesn't matter, Clay." Then she looked at him with a flirting smile. "We can always do it again."

He laughed and slid his hand between her legs, touching where he knew it pleased her most. She gasped. He laved her earlobe and whispered, "I'll make it feel good for you, too, then we can do it again later anyway.'' His guard was slipping way down, and he was too far gone to catch it.

When he stretched out on top of her, he thrust inside her. Then he stilled and kissed her eyes, her nose, her cheeks. She whimpered and tried to arch up into him.

He smiled as he kissed. "Not so fast. I want to do this nice and slow."

Her pulse at her throat fluttered. He watched her blue eyes, alight with silver sparks as he slowly pressed in deeper and then withdrew slowly...slowly...ever so slowly. She was quaking now, needing him the same way he needed her. With each deliberate coaxing thrust, he went deeper and deeper until she wrapped her legs around him, trying to hold him to her.

"This is going to be so good, Gina," he rasped into her neck.

Her voice shook as she responded, "It already is."

They both lost control. Their rhythmic movement became frenzied until Gina cried his name louder than he'd ever heard it. Clay's heart pounded and then roared in his ears as his shattering release took him so deep inside of her that they'd never forget what happened today.

He held her as their breathing returned to normal, as the sheen on their skin cooled them, as they fell back to reality.

When he raised himself up on his elbows, he gazed into her eyes. "I think you'd better inventory the closets today...or I'll never get this room papered."

As Gina pulled sheets, pillowcases and comforters from the closet, she understood another reason for

Clay's guardedness with her. He felt as if his father had forced him into marriage. She suspected there was anger toward his dad there that he wouldn't admit.

John McCormick had taken Clay's control of his own life out of his hands. Their wedding hadn't been much different from a shotgun wedding.

She thought about what had happened while they were wallpapering. Clay was a wonderful lover. He was in his prime…virile…and had sexual needs any woman would be glad to satisfy.

But he chose you, a hopeful voice reminded her.

"He didn't have anyone else to choose from," she muttered back, feeling like the solution to a problem, not a new bride.

Distracting herself from her thoughts, she emptied the top three shelves of the closet, then sat on the floor to pull out two cartons shoved in there. One of them was large and held extra blankets. When she pulled open the flaps of the one beside it, she realized it was only half-full. There was an old cigar box, a stack of maps, loose photographs. Curious, she studied the photographs and recognized Clay's father. He had his arm around a pretty brunette and she guessed the woman was Clay's mother.

Dipping into the box, she pulled out another fistful of photographs and this time found some of a small boy who was maybe four. In other pictures, six or eight. It was Clay. She could tell from the cheekbones, his nose, the set of his eyes. There were several of him climbing up a mountain, a few of him fishing, still others with him standing in front of an apartment building with his parents. The earliest ones were the happiest ones. Both John McCormick and his wife had changed over the course of the years, looking more serious.

When Gina heard Clay's boots as he came out of the bedroom, she looked over at him. Their gazes met and he glanced down at what she'd found.

"Did you know these were here?" she asked.

When he didn't immediately answer, she said, "I'm sorry I went through them."

He shrugged, "It doesn't matter. I should have thrown them out a long time ago."

"Why? You can't throw out these pictures. They're your history."

Stooping, he plucked the cigar box from the floor and opened it. Inside there was a collection of rocks and a leather pouch. Clay opened the pouch and spilled marbles into his hand.

"The past doesn't matter anymore. My dad couldn't bear to look at the pictures of him and my mom. It hurt him too much. That's probably why he shoved them in here instead of in his room."

"He must have missed you terribly when your mother took you away." Gina thought about the bond she'd seen between Clay and his father, and her heart ached for the years they'd lost.

"I think he kept thinking she'd come back to him…that she'd bring me back. That never happened."

"How old were you when you returned?"

"Sixteen. Dad gave me up so she'd go back to Illinois and get sober. He knew she was only drinking because she was so unhappy here. It worked. She did sober up when we went to Chicago. But I hated it. Her father was very much like your dad. He was a lawyer and he said if Dad didn't let her keep me, he'd get her sole custody. My father didn't want me to be a pawn in a game nobody could win. He flew to see me once a year but that wasn't nearly enough.''

''Your mother let you go freely when you were sixteen?''

''She'd remarried by then. I'd never gotten along with my stepfather. She couldn't stop me from leaving.''

''Is your mom still living?''

''No. She died five years ago—a heart condition she never knew she had.''

''You kept in contact with her?''

''She was my mother. I cared about her even if I didn't want to live with her. Those years she'd been drinking had driven a wedge between us. I called her every few weeks, but we never had much to talk about.''

So different from the bond that Gina had witnessed between Clay and John McCormick. No wonder he'd missed his father so desperately. No wonder he'd returned.

Clay had closed the cigar box, set it inside the carton and motioned to the pictures. ''They don't matter anymore. You might as well throw all of it away.''

Gina knew better than to do that. Clay may think that the past was dead, but his memories of that time mattered very much and possibly kept him from loving her now.

A week later, Gina had all the lights lit in the kitchen and dining area as she mixed up batter for gingerbread, worrying about how Clay was going to take her news. They only had daylight from about ten to three now. She was getting used to it, turning on more lights to replace the sunlight. Of course, it wasn't the same, but it would have to do. She tried to imagine what the reverse would be like come summer when there would be twenty hours of daylight, then realized she was just trying to play games in her mind to distract her from what she'd found out today.

This morning she'd realized her period was a week late. She was never late. As she had the night of the dance and a few other times, she'd felt queasy on and off, but just attributed it to all the changes in her life. She'd also felt a little dizzy now and then and thought she might be coming down with the flu. When she put those symptoms together with her calendar this morning, she'd gone into Fairbanks and bought a pregnancy test. It was positive. As she'd stared at the plus sign on the stick, she hadn't been shocked but overwhelmed with joy. She was going to have Clay's baby! On the heels of that, she remembered his stipulation. *If you get pregnant and you leave Alaska, the child stays with me.* That wasn't an issue as far as she was concerned. She loved Clay. She had no intention of leaving. But what if he didn't want her after the year. What then?

She was just pulling the gingerbread from the oven when she heard the garage door open. A few minutes later Clay came into the kitchen. When he looked at her, there was a complexity of emotions on his face, as if he wanted to take her into his arms the moment he saw her. Yet something prevented him from doing that.

"Hi," she said lightly, placing the gingerbread on a rack on the counter.

He took off his parka and hung it on the coatrack. "The kitchen smells good."

"I thought you might like something sweet with the roast."

"Whatever you make is always good. I'm going to get a shower before dinner."

"Clay, can we talk first?"

Stopping midway across the kitchen, he studied her, then agreed, "All right. Do you want to go into the living room?"

She knew it was anxiety, but she was feeling a bit shaky. "Yes, that would probably be a good idea."

He didn't sit beside her on the sofa but across from her in the recliner and looked anything but relaxed. He looked as if he was preparing himself for something. Maybe he thought she wanted to leave. Far from it.

Clasping her hands in her lap, she plunged in. "I don't know how to say this, Clay, except to just say it. My period is late so I went into town for a pregnancy test today. I'm pregnant."

For a moment he looked perplexed, as if he'd expected something entirely different. Then he grinned. "You're sure?"

"I can use another pregnancy test if you'd like, but they're pretty reliable these days from what I hear."

His grin slipped away. "How do you feel about it? This wasn't in the plans. That one night we weren't careful—"

"I've always wanted to be a mother. I didn't expect to be one quite this soon, but I'm happy about it. Are you?"

He closed his eyes for a moment as if he was analyzing the repercussions of a pregnancy. "I've always wanted children. But we had an agreement to stay married only for a year. We'll have to look at this marriage differently if a child's involved.''

"Yes, we will. Because a child needs both parents.''

His gaze locked to hers. ''Does that mean you'll consider staying longer than a year?''

Was that hope she heard in his voice? She had to be very careful. She knew he wasn't ready to hear about her love when he didn't even trust her yet. She had to prove she could be trusted; she had to prove she didn't want to be any place other than with him. Clay was the type of man who believed in actions, not words.

"I think if we're going to have a baby we should raise him or her together. Don't you?''

"A child should be able to count on both parents.''

They were skirting the issue of their relationship, but Gina couldn't force Clay to feel something he didn't. A child would give them a common goal.

"I'm sure Mary Lou can give you the name of her obstetrician,'' Clay suggested. ''You should make an appointment as soon as you can.''

"I'll call her after supper. I didn't want to tell anybody until I told you.''

He stood then and came over to sit beside her. ''You *are* happy about this?'' He gazed into her eyes as if he was trying to look so deep inside of her she couldn't tell him anything but the truth.

"I'm happy about this.''

"But what about your dreams? The tea room? The money I offered you will still be yours even if we stay married.''

Although Gina had been glad about the baby, glad Clay would have a reason to want her to stay, now she realized how complicated that was. Clay was the type of man who took all of his responsibilities seriously. If staying together was the best thing for the baby, that's exactly what he'd do whether he truly wanted it or not. She'd thought this baby might make it easier for Clay to love her. Now she wasn't so sure. The baby would be a reason he'd be tied to her. This marriage of theirs kept getting more and more complicated.

She said what he might want to hear. "I'd like to open the tea room some day. I'd like to have my own business. After all, this is the twenty-first century and women can do more than be mothers."

"I guess they can. I guess women still want independence even when they're mothers."

She'd hoped her answer would reassure him that he didn't have to bear all the burden, that she'd be fine on her own if it came to that. It would hurt her desperately, but if Clay only wanted their child and didn't want her at some point, she could stay close by and give him full access to his child. That didn't have to be settled now…nothing could be settled now. Only time would give them direction.

"Why don't you take your shower and I'll get supper out?" she asked. Then knowing there was one place where she could hope Clay's feelings for her would grow, she suggested, "We could celebrate by having dessert in bed."

"Gingerbread kisses," he said with a smile. "Sounds good to me. I'll be down in five minutes." He stroked her cheek, tipped her chin up to him and kissed her lightly on the lips, a tantalizing promise of what would come later.

Maybe they could make plans for the holidays, too. Maybe that would bring them closer. She could only pray something would.

* * *

After Clay adjusted the bedside lamp to the lowest setting, he picked up his grandfather's diary. He looked down at Gina whose back was pressed against his side. She'd fallen asleep after they'd made love. He remembered Greg saying how tired Mary Lou had been throughout her pregnancies. Clay guessed Gina's body was preparing for the life she was carrying. His child's life. He still couldn't quite wrap his mind around it. He'd been excited when she'd told him, near to jubilant. Yet on the heels of that buoyant feeling, he'd remembered their agreement. Would a baby keep Gina here? When he'd come home tonight and she'd so seriously asked if they could talk, he'd expected her to tell him she was leaving.

Clay thought about his own childhood, his mother's unhappiness. His father had told him his mother had never accepted the extremes of Alaska—the swings from almost total darkness to all-day light, the ninety degree summers to the subzero winters, the expense of simple things like eggs and beef. At least Elizabeth had admitted how darkness depressed her, how cold dried out her skin, how she disliked him working with the seasons, never sticking to a regular schedule. Could Gina cope with all that?

As Gina stirred in her sleep, Clay brushed a curl from her cheek. She seemed so young, so vulnerable, so exquisite. He wanted her all over again. He needed to focus on something else.

Opening the diary, he read the next entry:

February 24, 1931
    I hate to leave Cora alone. I don't even know how long I'll be gone. But Bear Creek has been

hit with an influenza epidemic.

They need supplies and I can take them. Cora insists she'll be fine. She has friends here if she needs anything. Still...

She's such a strong woman.

As Clay read the next entry, he learned his grandfather had been gone for three weeks. And when he returned:

March 25, 1931

I'm grinning from here to next year. Cora's going to have a baby. *We're* going to have a baby. It's early, but we've already chosen names. John Robert McCormick for a boy in honor of her father, Sarah Elaine McCormick for my mother. The baby will be born at the end of October, Cora tells me. She seems to know about these things and she's happier than I've ever seen her. I can't wait till October.

Clay could understand exactly how his grandfather felt. Already he wanted to know if he and Gina were having a girl or a boy. Would he or she look like him or Gina? What would he feel the first time he held the baby in his arms?

Maybe because his own child's birth seemed so far away, Clay needed to know what his grandfather had felt, and he read quickly through the next few months of entries. Alfred spoke of the ice on the river breaking up, of Cora's preparations for the baby. She was making blankets, sewing booties—little moosehide booties no bigger than his palm. The heat of summer bothered her and he kept a smudgepot burning to ward off the mosquitoes.

Finally October came. But the next few pages were blank! Did the diary stop here?

Clay kept turning the yellowed pages until he finally found an entry on December 8, 1931:

> Life as I know it has ended. The eternal darkness filling the days is filling my life. Cora died seven weeks ago. It wouldn't have happened if we had lived Outside. It wouldn't have happened if we'd lived somewhere where she could have gotten medical care. It was my fault for bringing her here. After the baby came, she began hemorrhaging. I lost her. I can't look at my son without seeing her, and I ache so deep I think I'll die. But I can't. I have to raise John...alone.

Clay's gut clenched. His chest became tight and he realized how much he identified with his grandfather.

Suddenly Gina awakened and sat up quickly. Before Clay could ask her what was wrong, she slid out of bed and ran to the bathroom.

Tossing the diary to the nightstand, he pushed himself across the bed and hurried after her. She'd shut the door, and he could hear her being sick inside. She might want privacy, but he wasn't going to give it to her right now. He had to make sure she was okay.

When he opened the door, he saw her sitting on the floor, her head in her hands.

"Go away, Clay," she mumbled.

"I'm not going anywhere. You're pregnant with my child, I'm going to take care of you."

She shook her head. "It was the gingerbread."

He took a washcloth from the rack and turned on the cold water. "I doubt that," he said wryly. "I think it more has to do with you being pregnant."

She gave him a weak smile. "I guess I've been lucky so far."

Squeezing out the washcloth, he went over to her and to her surprise, scooped her up into his arms and carried her to the bed.

"What are you doing?" she asked as her arms went around his neck.

"Keeping you from getting motion sickness." Actually he just wanted to hold her, to protect her and keep her safe. He settled in the bed with her on his lap and held the cloth to the back of her neck. "Is that better?"

"Much." She relaxed against him.

As he stroked her hair, he remembered the final entry in his grandfather's diary. "You're going to make that doctor's appointment tomorrow," he reminded her.

"Yes," she murmured, her head against his shoulder.

He rested his chin in her hair. She was going to take care of herself. She was going to get any medical attention she needed. He'd make sure of that.

His arms tightened around her as she fell asleep against his chest.

Chapter Nine

Clay didn't stop too long to think about the decision he'd made the following morning as he sat at the desk in the lodge, intent on composing an ad for a lodge manager. Maybe it was the influence of his grandfather's diary. Last night when he'd carried Gina to the bed, he'd never felt so protective of anyone. This morning when she would have gotten up with him, he'd insisted she sleep late. There was absolutely nothing she had to do...nothing that couldn't wait. With his air charter service slower now during the winter, he could keep a watchful eye on her and make sure she didn't overdo things. Hopefully they'd have a new manager by spring. It had taken seven months before Gina had answered their ad.

It was almost ten when Gina came into the office and took off her parka, a sheepish smile on her pretty face. "I guess I *did* need the sleep. I feel great now, though. I made an appointment with Mary Lou's obstetrician. I called Dad, too."

"What did he say?"

"He's thrilled he's going to be a grandfather."

Clay was sure Wesley Foster *was* thrilled. And he'd certainly want a grandchild close by...as close by as he wanted his daughter.

Changing the subject, Gina came over to the desk. "What are you doing? I thought you might be upstairs sorting through your dad's things."

Clay had left his father's rooms untouched since the night he'd taken the diary. He knew he had to pack up the clothes as well as the papers, but he wasn't quite ready. "That can wait," he said.

She came over to the desk. "Are you getting together the bookwork for the year?"

"No, I'm writing up an ad for a lodge manager. If we're lucky, we'll have one by spring and you can concentrate on being pregnant."

She looked shocked. "You're replacing me?"

"Gina, you're going to be a mother. I'm sure there are things you're going to want to do to prepare for that, and one of them isn't housekeeping chores—stooping, running up and down steps."

"Yes, I'm pregnant. But I'm going to be a mother, not an invalid. What do you expect me to do every day? Shop for baby clothes?" The color in her cheeks was high.

"You can shop, you can cook, you can read. Most of all you can rest," he said with confidence, knowing he'd made the best decision for her.

"Why didn't you consult me about this?"

"I never thought about consulting you. I'm just doing what's best for you." The ring of the words sounded familiar to his ears.

Her eyes were bright and sparkling with silver now,

and she was obviously piqued as she flung at him, "That's something my father would say!"

He had the feeling he was stepping into dangerous territory. "Lightening your workload has nothing to do with your father."

"Making my decision for me does. Why can't you trust my judgement to tell you if I need help? I need something fulfilling to do. I can't sit around for nine months with my feet up on a step stool. That isn't my idea of having a life."

He hadn't wanted to upset her. Now he stood and placed his hands on her shoulders. "You're exaggerating," he said gently.

"No, you're being controlling! I don't need that from a husband."

Clay could see tears well up in her eyes, but before he could do anything about it or say anything more, she pulled away from him and tossed over her shoulder, "I'm going to dust upstairs." Then she fled the office.

Now what in the hell was he supposed to do?

Gina ran up the stairs, her vision blurry from the tears. It had taken every ounce of her energy to keep her from blurting out that what she needed wasn't a lightening of her workload, but rather Clay's love. Did he think his role as a husband was to take over her life?

She did *not* want a man controlling her as her father had…as he still wanted to. When she'd told him she was pregnant, he'd tried to convince her to come home for a few weeks. She knew he didn't want her there for a few weeks…but permanently. She didn't know if it was her hormones or her fear that Clay would never feel as deeply about her as she felt about him that was making her so upset. It wasn't like her.

Finding a dust rag in the closet, she ducked into the first bedroom and frantically began cleaning.

Less than five minutes later, she heard Clay's footsteps in the hall. She didn't want to talk. She didn't want to start crying in front of him.

When he came into the room, she ignored him and kept dusting, hoping he'd see she was busy and just go away. But she should have known Clay wouldn't be deterred easily.

"Gina," his voice was firm.

Still she ignored him.

She was dusting the washstand sitting by the window when he came over to her and wrapped his arms around her. "Let's talk."

Pulling away from his chest, not giving in to the protection of his arms, she insisted, "We should have talked before you made the decision about the ad." Lodge manager was her job, and he'd just taken it away from her. It was just another way of him saying he didn't expect her to stay...or to be strong enough to be a partner in their lives. Her emotions were in an uproar and Clay's strength around her didn't help. She wanted too badly just to rest against him. She wanted too badly to tell him he'd become her world and his lack of confidence in her hurt her deeply.

Disregarding her words, he pulled her a little tighter against him a second time. "I want to take care of you. I want you to take care of yourself." Tenderly, he laid his hand over her stomach.

She took a deep breath because she loved his touch so much. She loved *him* so much.

He went on, "Come spring—by the time we hire

somebody—you'll be six months pregnant. I want to do everything I can to make that easy for you."

Those weren't the words Gina wanted to hear. Yet maybe his feelings for her and the baby were driving his concern. Clay wasn't like her father. He didn't need the upper hand just to make himself feel powerful.

Trying to get a handle on everything she was feeling, trying to be reasonable, she stopped resisting him. "Can't we wait until after the holidays to put the ad in the papers? Can't I think about it until then?"

He brushed his chin across her crown, then rubbed his cheek against her temple. "We can wait until after New Year's. By then we'll have to make real plans, including turning the spare room into a nursery."

A nursery. They would be planning that together, and each decision they made would bind them closer together. Clay would realize she had no intention of going anywhere ever…that she wanted to be married to him for the rest of their lives. Maybe then he could let himself feel again and trust again and hope again.

She closed her eyes and gave herself up to the pleasure of being held by the husband she loved…and prayed he'd come to love her.

It was December fourteenth, and Gina had so many things she wanted to do for Christmas—bake cookies, decorate the house, plan a party and invite Mary Lou and Greg, Joanie and Dave, Paul and his wife. There had been guests for the weekend at the lodge, an older couple and newlyweds on their honeymoon. The honeymooners had only come out of their suite for meals. As Gina cleaned the guest rooms in the lodge, she wished she and Clay could have a honeymoon. She reminded herself to be satisfied with what she had with Clay. She always smiled when she thought about the baby coming.

Fatigue set in as she returned home to cook supper. She made a stop in the bathroom to freshen up. When she did, she panicked. She was spotting…enough to worry her, enough to urge her to call Clay who was in his father's suite at the lodge. He answered his cell phone on the first ring.

"Clay, it's me."

"Did you forget something?" he asked, and she could hear the amusement in his voice. He'd just seen her five minutes ago when she'd told him she was returning to the house to start supper.

"I'm spotting, Clay. I'm going to call the doctor." She knew her voice was trembling but she couldn't help it.

"I'll be right over." He was as controlled as always, but underlying his words was the panic she felt.

She was still on the phone with the doctor when Clay came into the kitchen. Gina covered the receiver. "Dr. Barnett's at the hospital. She wants me to meet her there."

"We're on our way," Clay said, tension edging his eyes. He brought her her parka. After Gina hung up the phone, he asked, "Are you having any cramping?"

"The doctor asked me that, too. No, I'm not. She says that's a good sign."

As he helped Gina into her coat, he zippered it for her. His fingers still on the tie at her neck, he looked down at her. "It's going to be okay."

Tears came to her eyes, and she knew he could hear them in her voice. "I hope so."

Taking her into his arms then, he held her tight for a few moments. "Come on, let's go."

Their drive to the hospital in Fairbanks was tense. Neither wanted to talk about their fears or their hopes, or what would happen to them if something happened to the baby. Once Clay reached over to her, held her hand for a few minutes, then gazed back at the road. She wished she could read his thoughts. She wished she knew what was going on in his head. But then she never really knew.

The Emergency Room was fairly quiet and after registering, a nurse took them back to a cubicle to see the doctor.

Dr. Barnett was a woman in her fifties with steel-gray hair and gold-rimmed glasses. She was at least five-ten and could look imposing with her hair drawn back and her serious brown eyes. Clay had insisted on staying with Gina, and she was glad. Throughout the examination, her husband stood stoically looking out the window until the doctor was finished. Then he came to Gina's side and took her hand as she sat up on the table. "What's going on, Doctor?"

Doctor Barnett took off her glasses and gazed kindly at both of them. "Bleeding this early in the pregnancy doesn't mean anything is wrong. From all you've told me—you don't have cramps, you're not nauseous, you don't have a fever—it could be just a matter of course. So this is what I want you to do. Go home and rest. Keep your activities light over the weekend. You don't have to stay in bed, but don't do any cleaning or lifting or anything like that. Cooking's fine as long as it's just for the two of you and not for a party,'' she advised with a smile.

Patting Gina's shoulder, she suggested, "Call me on Monday and give me an update. Of course, if at any time anything changes, if the bleeding becomes heavier or you begin cramping, or anything else seems different, phone me immediately. You have my pager number. Do either of you have any questions?''

"There's nothing we can do?" Clay asked. "I mean medically."

"I know my advice makes you feel powerless, Mr. McCormick, but we have to gauge what nature's going to do. I don't see any indications of trouble, but we'll remain watchful."

Gina saw the troubled look on Clay's face, and she squeezed his hand. He squeezed back, and she felt closer to him than she'd ever felt before.

Still, they rode home in silence.

After Clay parked in the garage, they went into the kitchen and removed their coats.

His voice was gruff as he said, "I want you to do something for me."

"What?"

"Help me not feel so powerless. I know the doctor said you didn't need bedrest, but for this evening at least, that's where I'd like you to stay."

It was a simple thing he was asking. Resting in bed instead of staying occupied might make her worry more, though. "Are you going back over to the lodge?"

Shaking his head, he said, "Not a chance. I'm going to make you supper."

She smiled at that. "I didn't know you could cook."

"A man doesn't reach thirty-four years of age without knowing how to survive in the kitchen—at least on a small scale. Besides, I think we have leftovers in the refrigerator so I can cheat."

She actually laughed at that.

Coming close to her, he brushed the back of his knuckles against her cheek. "I'm going to take care of you, Gina."

"That sounds good," she whispered.

There was more in his eyes than desire now. It seemed like a deep caring. She knew he was concerned for the baby.

Then he swept her up into his arms. "Your resting begins right now." Lightly kissing her on the forehead, he carried her up to their bedroom.

Not only did Clay bring Gina supper, but afterwards he climbed in bed beside her and kept her company. They did something rare for them. He turned on the small TV and held her close by his side with his arm around her while they watched it. There were Christmas specials that made the time pass a little faster. When a new young talent beautifully sang one of Gina's favorite Christmas carols, she couldn't keep tears from trailing down her cheeks.

Clay held her close. "What's wrong?"

"Nothing's wrong exactly. Christmas just does that to me, I guess. It makes me feel more of everything."

"Are you going to miss not being with your father this year?"

Although her dad had always been busy and as she became an adult she had been too, holidays were sacred to them. Probably because her mother had always enjoyed them so thoroughly, they'd tried to keep up the practice. Usually they'd spent them to-

gether. Thanksgiving, Christmas and Easter were particular days that Gina knew her father would really
be there.

Thinking about him spending the holiday alone this
year made her heart ache. She didn't want him to be
lonely. "Dad said he didn't know what he was doing
for Christmas. I'm just hoping he finds someone to
spend it with."

Clay looked down at her for long moments. "You
miss him, don't you?"

"He's my father, Clay. Even though we don't
agree on mostly everything," she said with a small
smile, "I do love him."

At her response, Clay was silent.

"Did you and your father always agree on everything?" she asked.

"He was my best friend," Clay said in a husky
voice. "When we didn't agree, we talked it out."

"Christmas will be tough for you this year. I remember the holidays after my mom died."

"I'll think of the baby. Hopefully Dad will be
watching over us, helping things go the way they
should."

She liked that thought. She liked the idea of John
McCormick being their guardian angel.

When Clay was nearby, Gina felt that everything
would be all right...especially when he was holding
her. But by Sunday afternoon, the spotting still hadn't
stopped. Clay was looking more worried than ever
and her fears wouldn't keep still.

Finally she said to him, "Why don't you go do
what you have to do. I'll be fine here. Really. I'll take
a nap."

Cocking his head, he studied her warily. "Are you sure you won't try to make supper if I leave? Believe me, I can fry hamburgers with the best of them."

Trying to lighten the atmosphere between them, she teased, "I think I'll supervise, and we'll broil them."

"This pregnancy means I'll have to eat healthy food too, doesn't it?" He narrowed his eyes and looked as if the thought repulsed him.

She laughed. "It probably does. But at the end of nine months, you won't have gained twenty-five or thirty pounds."

"You'll still look great to me," he said sincerely as if he knew she might be worried about it.

Right now she was just worried about getting to the nine months. "I'll see about that when it happens," she responded quietly.

As if he could read her mind, he was quick to reassure her, "It'll happen."

But she was scared, and she just nodded. "Go on now. I'm sure there are lots of things you want to do over at the lodge or at the hangar."

"I'll stay at the lodge," he said firmly. "You call me if you need me."

"I will."

Pulling her into his arms, he gave her a thoroughly deep kiss and she melted against him not wanting him to go after all. She wouldn't tell him that, though. She didn't want him to feel trapped or fenced in in any way.

Gina really did intend to take a nap. But as she lay under the spread for at least a half hour, she couldn't quiet her mind. Trying to distract her thoughts from the baby, she planned what cookies she'd make and where they might put the Christmas tree. From that, her thoughts jumped to her father again. She missed him. He might be domineering and overprotective, but he did care and he was the only father she had.

Throwing back the covers, she slid her legs over the side of the bed and picked up the phone on the nightstand. Her dad was probably at his home office. She'd try him there.

He picked up the phone on the first ring. "Foster," he snapped.

"Hi, Dad."

"Gina! I'm glad you called. I was just trying to decide which bank to use for the trust fund for the baby."

"Dad, don't."

"What do you mean, 'don't.' This is my grandson or daughter. I'll pull out all the stops on this one."

She shook her head and sighed. Before he got carried away, before his enthusiasm knew no limits, she'd better tell him what was going on. "Please wait on that."

He must have heard something in her voice. "Why? What's wrong?"

"Nothing's wrong. Not really. That's what the doctor says. I'm spotting a little."

"Are you on bedrest?"

"Not quite. But Clay's insisting I do a lot of resting."

"Well, I should hope so. I think you should fly home immediately."

"I'm not coming home, Dad."

"Gina, the medical facilities here are superior. You know that."

"I'm getting good care here. Honest I am. The doc-

tor said all we can do is wait a few days and see if
the spotting stops.''

''And if it doesn't?''

''I'm taking this one day at a time. So should you.
I don't want you making plans and then if something
happens…'' Her voice caught and she stopped.

There was silence.

''You put yourself in that bed, Gina, and you don't
get up. When do you talk to the doctor again?''

''Tomorrow.''

''I want you to call me after you speak with her.
You let me know exactly what she says and exactly
what happens.''

''Why don't I wait and call you at the end of the
week.''

''Tomorrow, Gina.''

''All right. I'll call you tomorrow evening at
home.''

His voice gentled. ''McCormick's treating you all
right?''

''Clay's been great, Dad. He's even cooking,'' she
said with a small laugh.

''Is he there now?''

''No, I told him I was going to take a nap and he
should go get some work done.''

''But you're not napping.''

''No, I'm not. I'm talking to you. My mind is going
a mile a minute. You know how that is. Besides…
with Christmas coming and all…I missed you.''

''Finally,'' he mumbled.

''You act more like the Grinch than Santa sometimes, but I do know you care about me. Do you have
plans for Christmas yet?''

"I'm still thinking about it."

"Don't wait too long. Everyone will be busy."

"Do you need anything?" he asked her. "Money... raspberry pies?"

Again she had to smile. "If you want to do something really elaborate, you can send me another raspberry pie for Christmas."

"You'll have raspberry pie and a lot more."

Now what had she done? "Don't go overboard. I'd better let you get back to work. I'm going to try that nap again."

"Take care of yourself and call me tomorrow evening."

"I will."

When she hung up, she felt torn between her old life and her new one. It wasn't that she wanted to go back to San Francisco. She didn't. Yet she *did* miss her father and she missed certain connections she'd had there. Still, Clay was her life now. He was what mattered. Somehow she'd prove that to him, and they'd have the kind of marriage she'd always dreamed of.

On Monday afternoon, the spotting stopped. At Gina's urging, Clay had driven into the hangar in Fairbanks in the morning and she called him there. He sounded greatly relieved. After she spoke with Clay, she called her doctor. When the doctor returned Gina's call, she told her to resume her activities but to still take it easy and to call if there were any changes.

Gina felt as if she were holding her breath.

Clay had insisted he would make supper for them, but she put a salmon loaf in the oven anyway.

When Clay came home and smelled it, he shook his finger at her. "You're still supposed to be taking it easy."

"I am. I mixed it in a bowl at the counter, Clay, and it weighed less than a pound."

With eyes narrowed, he took her in his arms for a hug. "All right. But I bet it weighed two pounds. I brought us something for dessert." He opened the bag he'd set on the table and produced a chocolate layer cake. "What do you think?"

"I think I'm going to enjoy dessert tonight."

When he kissed her, the kiss was filled with the passion that had always been there but with gentleness, too, because they knew they weren't going to act on it…not until she was sure everything was okay with the baby.

During supper, they shared companionable silence between bits of conversation and were eating slices of chocolate cake when they heard a vehicle outside.

"Are you expecting anyone?" Gina asked him.

"No. Maybe it's an unexpected guest. I left the sign on the lodge that anybody looking for a room should come here."

Gina waited in the kitchen while Clay went to the front door. She was licking the last bit of icing from her fork when her father strode into the room, Clay not far behind him.

She dropped her fork. "Dad! What are you doing here?"

"I came to convince you to come back to San Francisco with me."

She'd planned to call him tonight after supper. "The spotting stopped."

"Maybe for now. But you need to be somewhere

where there are top specialists in the obstetrics field. You have to think of yourself as well as your child. I chartered a jet. I'll have you back in San Francisco tomorrow, seeing the best man in the field. Then you can be sure nothing will happen to you or the baby.''

The last thing she wanted was for anything to happen to this baby. She was suddenly confused. What if her father was right? What if she *did* need a specialist? What if they could do something doctors here couldn't?

She glanced at Clay, and he had that remote look on his face that she hadn't seen for a while. ''Dad, I don't want to talk about this now. Clay and I will have to discuss it. Are you hungry? We just finished supper.''

Her father looked more stern than she'd ever seen him. ''I'm not hungry, Gina. I want this settled.''

His rock-solid determination rattled her. ''It's not black and white. It's not as easy as hopping on a plane and going back to San Francisco.''

The telephone rang and Clay said tersely, ''I'll get it in the living room.''

She wanted to run to her husband, throw her arms around him, and ask him to help her make the decision that would be best for all of them. But he was already leaving the kitchen.

She looked over at her father.

Crossing to her, he put his arms around her in a gesture of affection he hadn't manifested in years. ''I'm worried about you and the baby. Don't you want the best possible chance to keep this child?''

Closing her eyes, Gina was more confused than she'd ever felt. Clay might have been tender and gentle with her the past few days, but he still hadn't told her how he felt about her. He still hadn't said he loved her. Maybe she was a naive fool to think he ever would. He'd been forced into this marriage to secure his inheritance. Why did she ever think feelings would eventually go with that? Just because *she* had them didn't mean he did. She'd thought desire could turn into love, but possibly she'd been wrong about that, too. Maybe desire was just what it was—lust and physical need.

As Clay went to answer the phone, he couldn't help but hear Wesley Foster's question. Didn't they *both* want Gina to have the best possible chance to keep this child?

Distracted, he picked up the receiver. To his surprise, the voice he heard was Jed's. "I need an antibiotic, Clay, and I need it as soon as you can fly it up."

"What's wrong?"

"It's one of my patients. She's not responding to any of the antibiotics I've given her. I called the pharmacist I use in Fairbanks. He has the drug I want. If you pick it up and fly it up, I might be able to save her."

"Give me the information. I'll radio what time I'll be there, and Harry can have the fire pots on the runway."

A few minutes later after Clay made a phone call, he returned to the kitchen and saw Gina, her father's arm still around her. "I have to fly to Deep River."

"Now?" Foster asked critically. "You shouldn't be leaving Gina alone."

"After I spoke to Jed, I called Mary Lou. She said you can stay with her and Greg if you'd like."

"You're not farming my daughter off on someone

else! I'm staying right here until she decides to come home with me.''

"Gina?" Clay asked his wife.

"I…I don't know, Clay. Dad's been making some good points. I don't want anything to happen to our baby.''

Clay vividly remembered the entries in his grandfather's diary—his grandmother, who had been a strong woman, dying in childbirth. He couldn't let anything happen to Gina. Yet if she returned to San Francisco, he knew her father would keep her there. He knew she'd never return.

Turmoil over all the feelings that had been building since they'd married, frustration and anger that she didn't trust what they could have *or* the doctor in Fairbanks, pushed words out of his mouth. "Go back to San Francisco with your father, Gina. You don't belong here. You never did.''

She looked torn. "But what about your dad's will? We have to…''

Clay brushed it off as if the will didn't matter anymore. "You'll have a child instead of $50,000. I'm not going to hold you here.''

"But you said—''

"Any discussion about our child right now is premature. Go back to San Francisco. See what happens. When and if we have a baby, I'll talk about custody. I have to go into Fairbanks and get that medicine. I'm going to fly it up tonight.'' He took his parka from the coatrack.

Gina ran to him. "Clay, you can't go like this. We need to talk.''

He was numb. He looked at Gina's pretty face and couldn't imagine her not being at his house when he returned. Yet he knew if something happened to her or their baby, he'd never forgive himself.

"I think your father has said it all. Call me when you get settled in San Francisco. Then we'll decide what we're going to do next. This marriage was a mistake, and we both know it."

Turning away from her, he zipped his parka and left the house, leaving the marriage that had cost him more than he'd ever expected.

Chapter Ten

Guided by fire pots on the Deep River airstrip, Clay landed in the Cessna around midnight. Since Dave had been doing some work on the Seneca, it had been quicker to get the Cessna ready for takeoff. Clay hadn't wanted to lose any time getting to the village. After he tended to the plane, he headed for the clinic where Jed had told him he'd be—with his patient.

When Clay handed Jed the vial with the antibiotic, the doctor said gratefully, "This could make the difference between life and death, Clay. Thanks for getting it up here."

"No problem," Clay muttered, feeling as numb inside now as he had when he'd left home. He'd saved a life but ended his marriage. During preparations for the flight up here, he'd tried not to think about it. Yet during the flight, with black skies surrounding him, he'd felt as aimless as his plane would have been without the instruments to guide him to Deep River.

Gina was leaving. He couldn't fly far enough away from that thought.

Jed tossed over his shoulder, "Use my snow machine to go back to my cabin. You look beat. Will I see you before you fly out tomorrow? I hear weather's moving in."

"I don't know yet when I'm flying out. I'll talk to you before I leave."

Jed was already on the far side of the clinic attending to his patient.

Clay had driven Jed's snow machine before. It was a powerful one, and he was back at the cabin in no time flat. He got a fire going in the woodstove, then took out the bottle of rye Jed kept in a cupboard. Pouring himself three fingers, he decided to make the drink last.

Unbidden, thoughts of his childhood came tumbling through his head—his parents together, his mother in an alcoholic stupor at the end of each day, his father trying somehow to make it all right but unable to. He looked at his glass of rye, still two-thirds full, pushed himself up from the chair and poured it down the sink. Jed would have his head for pouring away good whiskey, but he knew better than to try to numb the pain. Pain was what pain was. He knew if he didn't feel it, it would eat him away.

He'd known Gina was going to leave. He'd never really expected her to stay. So why was the pain so intense? Why was it so much worse than when Elizabeth left?

Because Gina's carrying your child.

The words in his grandfather's diary haunted him. *It wouldn't have happened if we had lived Outside.*

Clay knew he had to let go of Gina and his baby

because that was what was best for them. Yet it hurt like hell, and he knew even sleep wouldn't make the torment go away.

All through the night he tossed and turned on the cot. His grandfather's written words, scenes from his own childhood, the last few years with his dad, played through his dreams. Like an angel hovering over all of it was Gina, her sweet face anguished, her eyes troubled as she'd listened to her father.

It was still dark when Clay awakened. In a few days on December twenty-first, the longest night would last about twenty-one hours. This was what most folks couldn't get used to—cycles of light and darkness shortening and lengthening, unusual rhythms, distinctive beauty that came with a cost. The thought of the mountains and the Northern Lights and the deep snows and the vibrant colors of summer almost haunted Clay now. His grandfather had loved Alaska and his wife had died. His father had loved it and he'd lost his family. Clay loved it. Did that mean he'd be alone the rest of his life?

He only knew one place he might find some answers. His father had been his best friend, but Ben had always been his mentor. Now he needed to talk to him.

When Clay stepped outside and climbed onto the snow machine, he could feel snow coming. If he got snowed in here, so be it. Gina would be gone when he got back. He was sure her father would whisk her away as soon as he could.

Clay showed up at Ben's door, and his older friend didn't seem surprised. "You didn't bring your wife with you?" Ben asked by way of greeting.

"My wife is leaving Alaska."

Ben studied Clay for a long moment, then motioned him inside. Many times over the years they'd forsaken the furniture and sat on cushions on the floor near the woodstove where Clay had spent long hours listening to Ben's stories, absorbing his wisdom. Now he didn't even know where to begin.

Before he could, Ben shocked him. "I know about your father's will."

"How could you know? Unless… Dad told you what he was going to do?"

Ben raised one knee and straightened his other leg in front of him. Then he leaned forward slightly. "Your father didn't want his son to end up a disillusioned, lonely man."

"A marriage in order to claim my inheritance was going to prevent that?" Clay's anger at his father was evident now and he knew it was time he admitted it.

Ben closed his eyes for a moment then leaned back and opened them. "Your father knew if you married again, you'd choose better the second time."

Clay felt himself flush. Elizabeth's blond hair, amber eyes and model's figure had blindsided him. It wasn't until after they were married that he realized her charm was just that, and it hid a selfishness he hadn't realized was there. "How did Dad think I was going to find a good marriage or a suitable wife when I had to do it because of a will? He knew I hadn't been dating seriously. He knew the planes and flying were all that mattered to me. Did he expect the perfect wife just to drop out of the sky?"

"He knew—" Ben agreed, pausing until he was sure he had Clay's full attention. "He knew that possibly the perfect wife for you was right under your nose."

The shock of it hit Clay like a blow. "Gina? He wanted me to marry Gina?"

"In our last conversation, your father told me he could easily think of Gina as a daughter." While Clay absorbed that, Ben sipped at a mug of coffee. When he'd replaced the mug on the floor, he asked, "Did you marry Gina simply because of your father's will?"

Clay remembered the first day he'd met Gina at the lodge. He remembered how her sweet beauty had wrapped itself around him slowly, how each time he'd seen her he'd been more attracted to her. Not the same way he'd been attracted to Elizabeth. Elizabeth's beauty had bowled him over. Some of it had even been artificial, and he hadn't realized that until he'd met Gina. Gina was innocence and vulnerability and freshness that he'd told himself for months he was too cynical to touch. Yet how he'd wanted to touch it…how he'd wanted to touch her. It had gone deeper than any desire he'd ever felt for a woman. And when she'd sat with him at his father's bedside, desire didn't begin to cover the connection he'd felt to her. Her compassion and caring had been something he'd craved even more than physical satisfaction.

That's why he'd married her.

"If Gina leaves, what are you going to do about your inheritance?" Ben asked.

Clay had thought about that during the night. "I'll start over. I'll get a job as a commercial pilot for a while until I can buy another plane." Then he shrugged. "Maybe I'll come up here and trap and fish like you do."

Ben shook his head. "You know the days of truly

living off the land are over. Man has made too much progress, done too much damage. Besides, my needs are simple.''

"So are mine."

"Are they?" Ben argued.

Clay's needs didn't seem so simple at this moment because what he needed was Gina. *Who* he needed was Gina. It didn't even have anything to do with the baby. He couldn't imagine going back to his house and Gina not being in it. He couldn't imagine sleeping alone at night. He couldn't imagine not seeing her sweet smile or hearing her lovely voice. He ached with the thought of her absence, hurt more than he'd hurt about anything, even his father's death. Maybe because he'd known his father's time had come. His time with Gina had just started.

''You've got a lot to think about,'' Ben said in his quiet way. ''Even more important, you have more to listen to. You have to let go of being taken away from your father when you were a child. You have to let go of your first marriage and how betrayed you felt. You have to let go of your anger over your father's will. If you do all that, and you truly listen to who you are and what you want, a simple message will echo with every beat of your heart. You'll find your life path again.''

Two hours later, Ben's words still playing in Clay's mind, he taxied down the runway and soared into the twilight sky. Twilight at midday. Alaska in his soul. Yet...

As he flew, trying to beat the weather front that was chasing his tail, he listened as Ben had instructed. When he experienced turbulence, he still listened.

Letting go was more difficult. Letting go wasn't as simple as flying out of clouds. It was more like flying into the center of the storm, being tossed to and fro, and then finding the calm in its wake.

Let go and listen.

Snow hit Clay's windshield, and air currents tossed the Cessna. He checked the instrument panel. Although he flew the Seneca most of the time, this plane was just as familiar to him. He climbed, trying to fly above the storm. As he took the plane higher, he could hear the message in his heart. *You love Gina. You will love her forever.* The insight was as startling as the storm that had chased Clay and finally caught him.

Suddenly the engine coughed.

At first he thought it was carburetor ice. He put the carburetor heat on. But the coughing didn't cease and on the instrument panel, he saw the fuel flow was reduced.

There was ice in the fuel lines. He had to take the plane down.

If he could just make it to Bear Creek and the field on the outskirts...

The wind buffeted him as he turned on the radio and sent a distress message. "Mayday... mayday...mayday. Cessna Skymaster November-1-7-1-7-Charlie. Losing engine power four miles from Bear Creek. One soul on board."

Snow swirled around him as he kept his eyes on the instrument panel. He knew he wasn't going to make it to Bear Creek.

Again he heard in his heart, *You love Gina. You will love her forever.*

The coughing in the engine increased. His hands

were tight on the yoke as he hoped his memory of the area would guide him since fire pots or runway lights wouldn't. The snow-covered ground came up to meet him before he was ready. As his plane hit a snowbank, he saw his father's face...and Gina's.

Then everything went black.

As Gina took the casserole of macaroni and cheese out of the oven Tuesday evening, her father came into the kitchen. He'd been on the phone most of the afternoon, taking care of business. But now he had that determined look on his face that she knew so well.

"Have you made up your mind yet? Are you going back with me?"

When she didn't respond right away, he went on, "Any marriage based on the terms of a will can never succeed. You can't think staying with this man is the right thing for you to do."

She plopped the casserole onto the table on the hotpad and held up her hand. "Stop it, Dad. Just stop it. I've listened to all your arguments, I've listened to all your good reasons. Truthfully, I see no difference making the agreement with Clay as I did, than you trying to arrange a marriage for me with Trent."

"I never arranged—"

"You did. You saw his interest in me and you took advantage of it. I'm sure he told you I heard the two of you talking. That *is* why I left San Francisco. I'm tired of doing things your way. Your way isn't necessarily what's right for me."

For once in her twenty-three years, her father didn't come right back at her with another argument. He studied her pensively. "Trent said you had no feelings for him and that's why you wouldn't consider marrying him."

She opened the drawer and took out a serving spoon. "That's right."

"Look at me, Gina."

Slowly, she faced her father.

He made a noise of disgust. "You think you're in love with this Clay McCormick. That's it, isn't it? That's why you married him. That's why you can't make up your mind to leave."

"Yes, I'm in love with Clay. But he doesn't love me. I don't know if he can ever really love any woman. I'm truly concerned about what kind of parents we'll be for our child if he doesn't love me. I know he'll be a good father, but I don't want to trap him. I don't want to ground him, and I don't want to be a burden he doesn't want."

She'd cried most of the night and gone over all of it in her head time after time after time. Her heart was telling her to stay, her mind was telling her to go. Since last evening when he'd arrived, her dad had played on all her fears and her concern for the life she was carrying within her.

When the phone rang, her heart leapt in hope that it might be Clay. Maybe he was calling asking her not to leave, to at least wait until he got back so they could discuss their future.

That was a pipe dream as she heard Jed's voice. "Hi, Jed." Then she wondered why Jed was calling if Clay was there in Deep River and her heart started beating faster. "What's wrong?"

"There's no easy way to say this, Gina. Clay's plane went down."

Everything in her world got fuzzy for an instant

and she caught the edge of the counter. Then she fought through the shock of Jed's words. "How do you know?"

"Clay radioed using the Anchorage Center frequency before he crashed or landed, we don't know which. A jet picked it up. No one's heard anything since but not many planes are flying tonight to pick up anything from him."

Terrible pictures played in Gina's mind, and she shut her eyes. That didn't help.

Her father crossed to her. "What's wrong?"

Putting her hand over the receiver for a moment, she choked out in a whisper, "Clay's plane went down."

Her father put his arm around her shoulders.

"Gina, I want you to listen to me," Jed said. "Clay's lived here long enough to know how to survive. He has provisions in his plane for an emergency like this."

"Is anyone looking for him?"

"No one can search until the storm lets up."

"That could be tomorrow!" According to the weather reports, they might get snow all through the night.

Jed's voice remained calm. "Yes, it could be tomorrow, but everyone's praying the snow'll stop sooner. We only have a general idea where Clay is from his message and his flight plan. The storm might have thrown him off course. They'll be looking for his Emergency Locator Transmitter."

"Oh, Jed."

"Do you have someone with you? Clay told Ben your father was there before he left."

She wondered what else Clay had said, what else

he had felt. When her father had suggested she return to San Francisco, she should have refused him outright, made her stand, proven to Clay that she wanted a life with him. He would have accepted her loyalty if not her love. She knew that now. So much was clear now.

"Yes, my father's still here."

"Paul will be out searching as soon as he can and so will every other pilot Clay knows. Your husband is an experienced pilot and a survivor. So you hold on. Do you hear?"

Her knees felt weak but she said firmly and clearly, "I hear. We'll all be praying for him."

"I'll contact you as soon as I know anything."

When she put down the receiver, her father squeezed her shoulders. "I have a friend in the FAA. I'll call him."

Taking a deep breath, Gina pulled herself together. "Use your cell phone if you can. I want to keep the line open. When you're finished, I need to use it to call a few of Clay's friends."

Her father looked at her as if he was surprised that she hadn't fallen apart. She wasn't going to fall apart. She had a vigil to keep.

The next few hours crawled by even though Gina kept herself busy speaking with Mary Lou and Greg, Murray and Joanie. They would all be praying with her. She drank tea, watched weather reports with her father...and prayed. She prayed harder than she'd ever prayed in her life.

It was almost 2:00 a.m. when her father came into the kitchen and found her drinking yet another cup of tea. "Don't you think you should go to bed?"

She turned down the radio with the "oldies but

goodies'' music and weather reports every fifteen minutes. The snow had stopped, and she hoped that meant searchers were looking for Clay. ''There's no point. I wouldn't sleep.''

''Still…'' her father said, about to argue with her.

The phone rang. Gina was out of her chair and snatching it up before her father could even think about answering it.

''Hello?'' she asked, not knowing who or what to expect.

''It's Jed, Gina.''

There was something about his voice that made her hold her breath. ''What?''

''Paul found Clay and is in radio contact with him. Clay had to make an emergency landing. It was pretty rough, and apparently he was knocked out for a while. But he's conscious now. He said he's all right. He has a thermal bedroll and battery operated lantern, water and trail mix, too, if he needs it. He can't fly the plane out. There was damage to the propellers. But we know where he is, and we're going to get him as soon as we can. I'm not sure where they're going to take him, though. It probably depends on what condition he's in when they go in to get him.''

''Jed…''

''He's tough, Gina. You know that. I'll be talking to Paul again, trying to monitor Clay's condition that way. So try not to worry.''

''Not worry?''

''Yeah, that was a stupid thing to say. I'll keep you informed on what's going on.''

''Thanks, Jed.''

''No thanks necessary.''

When Gina hung up, she looked at her father.

"He's alive. They'll go in and get him as soon as they can."

"He's fortunate."

"He's more than fortunate. He's an expert pilot."

"If he's such an expert, why did he head out in weather like this?"

That was an answer Gina didn't have. "I don't know. But I'm going to find out. I'm staying here, Dad. I'm not going anywhere. I want to be here when Clay gets home. As soon as the airport is opened, I want you to go back to San Francisco."

"But the baby…"

"I'm going to trust my doctor. Clay and I will make any decisions we need to make. Together."

Expecting her father to argue, Gina prepared herself, sure in her love for Clay, determined to nurture his caring for her until it developed into love.

To her surprise, her father pulled out a kitchen chair and sank heavily into it. "You've changed."

"Yes, I have." Her adventure into an unknown land had done that for her, giving her a growing sense of confidence in her own dreams. Her love for Clay and this baby had made her strong.

Now she'd wait for Clay and share her strength with him.

When Clay unlocked his front door on December twenty-first, he steeled himself against going into an empty house. After he'd been rescued and taken to Fort Yukon, the doctor there had stitched his forehead and held him for observation. Tired of care that seemed overzealous, Clay had insisted on flying back to Fairbanks this morning with a pilot coming that way.

Greg had picked him up at the airport and dropped him off at the house. Although his friend had offered to come inside with him, he'd waved Greg's concern away. His ribs were still sore but his head had stopped pounding. The ache down deep inside wouldn't go away with recuperation or the concern of a friend. It wouldn't go away until he saw Gina again and convinced her he loved her. He might have destroyed any chances he had the night he'd walked out. Sure he'd had to go. But not like that. Not in bitterness. Not in pain and anger because he was sure she would run back to the life she'd led before he'd met her.

All these months his feelings for Gina had deepened, and he'd kept calling it desire. He'd been afraid to call it anything else because then it would have power over him...*she* would have power over him. That thought had made him put up barriers, had made him deny intensely tender feelings that he'd attributed to the thought of a child. He loved Gina whether or not they had a child. If he'd only realized that sooner. Tonight was the longest night of the year and it might be the longest night of his life.

When he opened the door and stepped inside, he thought for a moment he was in the wrong house. It smelled of cinnamon and brown sugar. Tiny lights in a garland twinkled at him from along the mantel where a nativity scene sat. Next to it there was a photograph of Clay's father and of another woman he didn't recognize. She looked a lot like Gina. Was it her mother?

There was a huge brandy snifter of brightly colored shiny balls sitting on the table next to the sofa, a large red pillar candle on a crystal dish by the recliner, and in the corner of the room, by the window, stood a

Christmas tree decorated with popcorn and cranberry strands, iced shortbread cookies, and small velvet bows of every color and size.

What in blazes was going on?

"Hi, Clay."

Amazed by the sound of a voice he didn't expect to hear, he turned toward the kitchen.

Gina was dressed in black leggings and a long red sweater that almost came to her knees. She had a gold barrette in her hair, and her blue eyes were studying him as if she was afraid of his reaction in finding her there.

Damn. He felt like a first class idiot, and he didn't know where or how to begin. "You've decorated for Christmas," he said, not knowing what else to say.

She nodded and her gaze went to the bandage across his forehead, the bruises on his cheek. "Are you really all right? Jed said you were. But I've been so worried."

"I'm fine. I never expected you to be here. I thought you'd be back in San Francisco."

He saw her straighten her shoulders and lift her chin. "Do you want me to fly back to San Francisco?"

He knew what she was really asking him—did he want to continue with their marriage?

He dropped his duffel bag onto the floor and crossed to her. Taking her by the shoulders he knew he had to declare himself now or lose her. "I don't want you going anywhere…at least not without me. If you're concerned about the baby, or yourself, or you don't think you can stand life here, we'll move. I can fly anywhere—even in San Francisco."

She looked shocked. "You'd do that for me?" The

wonder in her voice touched him like nothing else could.

"I know I haven't given you reason to believe it, but I'd move heaven and earth for you if I could. I had lots of memories standing in my way, keeping me from saying what was right in front of my nose. I love you, Gina. I don't know how or when or why it happened, but it did, long before I knew it did. I guess my dad saw it."

He wrapped his arms around her and brought her close to him. "I want you with me for the rest of my life. Is that too much to ask? Did I destroy whatever we had by leaving the way I did? Do you think you can love me someday?"

With each of his questions, Clay saw more tears well up in Gina's eyes and he was afraid he was too late, he was afraid his pigheaded determination not to feel anything had ended their marriage before it had a chance to survive.

But then her arms circled his neck. "I love you, Clay McCormick. I should have told you before now. When your dad hired me and I met you, you were every dream I've ever had about what a man could be like. I saw how you cared about your father, how you treated the staff, how you flew off into the wild blue yonder like heroes I'd only read about."

"I'm no hero," he protested gruffly.

"To me you are. When you asked me to marry you, I was proud to say yes, proud to be your wife. But it didn't seem as if you really *wanted* a wife."

Loving the feel of her in his arms, beginning to believe she was truly his, he admitted, "I didn't have the courage to look at you as a wife. I'd seen what happened to my mother. And Elizabeth had taken off as if marriage vows hadn't been promises meant to be kept. But I promise you, Gina, if you give me the chance, I'll be the best damn husband you could ever want. I'll cherish you and protect you and love you every day of our lives."

The vows had come so easily...with all of his heart. He could see in Gina's eyes that she knew he meant them.

He kissed her then with all the passion that had been building since they'd married, with the fervor of his newly realized love, with the devotion of a man who intended to stay married for a lifetime. In their kiss, he felt Gina give him all she was, and all she could be. Neither held anything back and they held on to each other as if they were soaring into the blue sky of a brand new world.

Finally when they both needed to come up for air, Clay swung Gina into his arms and carried her to the sofa. His ribs didn't hurt a bit.

She snuggled against him, then gently caressed the bruises on his cheek. "I was so scared. I thought I might never see you again."

"When I was going down, I saw your face in front of my eyes and I knew I loved you. I knew I had to get back here to you. That's why I left Deep River when I did. I thought I could get back before you left."

"Oh, Clay," she sighed. "Dad kept pushing me to go back with him, and I kept resisting. I'm sorry I didn't refuse him the first time he asked. I'm sorry I didn't tell you then that I loved you and that I didn't want to go anywhere."

"We have to think of the baby."

"I *am* thinking of the baby. There hasn't been any

more spotting even through all this. I saw the doctor again yesterday and she said there's no reason why I shouldn't have a healthy baby. I trust her Clay. I trust the medical professionals here. I don't want to go anywhere. I want to stay here with you—through long nights and bright days and everything life deals out to us, including bears and snowstorms."

"I misjudged you," he said with deep regret. "I didn't trust the compassion and sense of responsibility that drew me to you in the first place. You have my grandmother's pioneer spirit, Gina. You're a rare breed of woman, and I can't believe you're mine."

"Believe it," she murmured as she kissed the bruise on his jaw. "Because I'll be yours forever."

Clay wrapped Gina more tightly into his arms, never intending to let her go.

Epilogue

One Year Later

When Clay stepped into the bedroom, he stopped, still awed by the sight of Gina nursing their five-month-old daughter, still awed by the depth of his love for both of them.

Gina gazed up at him with all the loving, tender feelings he always saw in her eyes. "She's almost asleep." She brushed their baby's fine, dark brown, curly hair across the top of her head with her fingers.

Sarah's hair was brown but her eyes were blue like Gina's. She was absolutely beautiful and he didn't know what he'd ever done to deserve such a gift...to deserve Gina. They both made life so full he couldn't comprehend it sometimes.

"The older she gets, the more her name fits her," Gina decided with a smile. "I'm so glad you suggested we name her Sarah Elaine, the name your grandparents picked out for a girl if they had one."

A year ago today Clay had returned home from his downed plane and his brush with death to find Gina waiting for him. He'd never expected that. He'd expected to have to move his life to San Francisco to court her and woo her as he should have done in the first place. In the weeks that followed they'd hardly spent a minute apart. Christmas had become more than a day on the calendar, and the beginning of the new year had brought them both a new life. They often took out his grandfather's diary and read it again as they had the first time during the long nights of late December.

"It *is* perfect for her," he agreed, sitting on the bed beside his wife. When he leaned down, Gina turned her face up to him and their kiss was long and leisurely and deep. She was flushed when he pulled away from her, and his heart was racing as it always did when he was close to her.

"I'll take Sarah to her room," he said, gazing down at their sleeping daughter. "Then there's something I want to get downstairs." As he lifted Sarah from Gina's arms he smiled and winked. "Don't go away."

Gina laughed and the sound followed him to his daughter's bedroom.

Last winter as Gina's pregnancy progressed, he'd wallpapered the room. Teddy bears danced around the border close to the ceiling. The crib and chest and bookshelves were light birch. The five-foot high stuffed giraffe in the corner had come from FAO Schwartz from Gina's father. He was flying in tomorrow to join them for the holiday. Clay and Wesley Foster had made their peace. They both wanted Gina's happiness and now Sarah's. That seemed to be all that mattered. He and Gina still had to stand firm when Wesley tried to run their lives, but the older man backed down when he saw he couldn't steamroll them. Clay felt Wesley respected them for their independence.

After Clay settled Sarah in her crib, he leaned down and kissed her soft baby cheek. She was a miracle…a miracle he'd never take for granted.

When Paul had returned from a flight to Seattle today, he'd brought something along for Clay that he'd kept in his car as a surprise. Now he went to fetch the bag. Stopping in the kitchen, he washed the large strawberries, dumped them into a bowl, then grabbed the canister of whipped cream from the refrigerator, mounded some into a dish, and carried it all up to their bedroom.

Gina was at the dresser brushing her hair. She was wearing a pale pink satin nightgown that was impractical in the winter, but perfect for raising his temperature enough to heat both of them.

"I have a surprise." His voice was husky. It always got that way when he looked at his wife and felt so many emotions they were too many to count.

She came flying toward him and wrapped her arms around his neck. "You wonderful man. Where did you get those?"

Before he spilled something, he set the bowls on the bed then lifted Gina into his arms. "Paul got them for me. I think we should start a tradition. We'll always feed each other strawberries and whipped cream on the longest night of the year."

Gina's blue eyes danced impishly as she said, "I think I like the longest night of the year better than the longest day."

Laughing, he swept her into his arms and carried her to their bed. They were going to spend the night recommitting themselves to each other. They did that every time they made love. Cupping her chin in his palm, he kissed her forehead, her eyes, her nose, then he leaned away. "I think you taste better than those strawberries ever will."

"And I still think you're the most wonderful man in Alaska."

Gina always made him feel as if he was her hero, her prince, her world.

Stretching out beside her, kissing her again, Clay knew she was his sunlight, his hope, a gift so precious that he'd spend the rest of his life making sure he deserved her.

"Let's turn off the light," she whispered close to his ear, "so we can really wrap ourselves up in the night."

Clay switched off the lamp then enfolded Gina in his arms. He vowed they'd always celebrate their longest night like this. If they did, their longest days would be memorable, too. Day or night, sunlight or darkness, snow or blue skies, they were together forever...together in love...together in an adventure that would bring them closer with each passing hour.

As Clay made promises to Gina and she whispered them back, the Alaskan night enfolded them into its mystery and beauty, and they loved each other into the new day and beyond.

* * * * *

Watch for Karen Rose Smith's
next Silhouette Romance in September 2002.

King Philippe has died, leaving no male heirs to ascend the throne. Until his mother announces that a son *may* exist, embarking everyone on a desperate search for... the missing heir.

Their quest begins March 2002 and continues through June 2002.

On sale March 2002, the emotional
OF ROYAL BLOOD
by Carolyn Zane (SR #1576)

On sale April 2002, the intense
IN PURSUIT OF A PRINCESS
by Donna Clayton (SR #1582)

On sale May 2002, the heartwarming
A PRINCESS IN WAITING
by Carol Grace (SR #1588)

On sale June 2002, the exhilarating
A PRINCE AT LAST!
by Cathie Linz (SR #1594)

Available at your favorite retail outlet.

Where love comes alive™

You've shared love, tears and laughter.

Now share your love of reading—

give your daughter Silhouette Romance® novels.

Silhouette®

Where love comes alive™

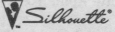